THE *Debutante* and the DUKE

SEDUCTIVE SCOUNDRELS

COLLETTE CAMERON

Blue Rose Romance®
Portland, Oregon

Sweet-to-Spicy Timeless Romance®

THE DUBUTANTE AND THE DUKE
Seductive Scoundrels
Copyright © 2020 Collette Cameron®
Cover Art: Kim Killion

Attn: Permissions Coordinator
Blue Rose Romance®
8420 N Ivanhoe # 83054
Portland, Oregon 97203

eBook ISBN: 9781954307414
Paperback ISBN: 9781954307421

collettecameron.com

"Nae more, *lèannan*.

"I canna control myself with ye.

"Ye are intoxicatin'. An irresistible aphrodisiac…"

Other Collette Cameron Books

Daughters of Desire (Scandalous Ladies)
A Lady, A Kiss, A Christmas Wish
Coming soon in the series!
No Lady for the Lord
Love Lessons for a Lady
His One and Only Lady

The Honorable Rogues®
A Kiss for a Rogue
A Bride for a Rogue
A Rogue's Scandalous Wish
To Capture a Rogue's Heart
The Rogue and the Wallflower
A Rose for a Rogue

The Blue Rose Regency Romances:
The Culpepper Misses
The Earl and the Spinster
The Marquis and the Vixen
The Lord and the Wallflower
The Buccaneer and the Bluestocking
The Lieutenant and the Lady

Highland Heather Romancing a Scot
Triumph and Treasure
Virtue and Valor
Heartbreak and Honor
Scandal's Splendor
Passion and Plunder
Seductive Surrender
A Yuletide Highlander

Castle Brides
The Viscount's Vow
Highlander's Hope
The Earl's Enticement
Heart of a Highlander (*prequel to Highlander's Hope*)

Seductive Scoundrel's
A Diamond for a Duke
Only a Duke Would Dare
A December with a Duke
What Would a Duke Do?
Wooed by a Wicked Duke
Duchess of His Heart
Never Dance with a Duke
Earl of Wainthorpe
Earl of Scarborough
The Debutante and the Duke
Wedding her Christmas Duke
Earl of Keyworth
Coming soon in the series!
How to Win A Duke's Heart
Loved by a Dangerous Duke
When a Duke Loves a Lass

Boxed Sets
Lords in Love
Castle Brides Collection: Books 1-3
The Honorable Rogues® Books 1-3
The Honorable Rogues® Books 4-6
Seductive Scoundrels Series Books 1-3
Seductive Scoundrels Series Books 4-6
The Blue Rose Regency Romances:
The Culpepper Misses Series 1-2

Dedication

This book is for all of the kind
souls who seek the good in others.

Who don't gloat or take satisfaction
when misfortune befalls others.

Who strive to take the high road, even when
surrounded and targeted by those less decent.

And who stand for truth and integrity,
no matter the consequences.

Thank you for being people of noble character.

I salute you.

1

17 Bedford Square
London, England
2 June 1810

Singing softly, Rayne Wellbrook gently swung the heavy wicker basket she held. She skirted the fountain burbling in the center of the paved circle bordered by a quartet of stone benches in her aunt and uncle's elaborate gardens.

Between each ornate bench, marble statues of Greek goddesses and gods stood as majestic, silent guardians. Ribbons of morning sunlight cast them in luminous golden hues and gave each an ethereal appearance.

"I sow'd the seeds of love," Rayne sang a little louder.

"And I sow'd them in the spring,

"I gather'd them up in the morning so soon…"

Mama had been an opera singer until she married Papa and had instilled a love for singing in Rayne from the time she was able to speak. Mama and Grandmama had been gone for nine years now—Papa far longer. Rayne couldn't even remember her soldier father.

Closing her eyes for a long blink, she filled her lungs with the sweet fragrances of jasmine, peonies, roses, and other vibrant summer blossoms festooning the zealously maintained pathways. Patches of lush green grass complemented the fastidious flower beds—each diligently attended by the cheerful gardeners the duke employed.

Mostly cheerful, that was.

All except for the fussy, meticulous head gardener.

Heaven forbid that Fitzroy—the surly curmudgeon—should find a single insolent weed or impertinent spent blossom amongst *his* beloved lower beds. The wizened, stoop-shouldered man even groused when the *"damned impudent birds"*—his words, not Rayne's— used *his* fountains as birdbaths.

In point of fact, he objected when they used the birdbaths as *birdbaths*.

At present, a pair of bluish-black feathers floated in the middle layer of the fount's rippling water. Those avian offenders bespoke an early morning dip by a cheeky crow or raven, as the otherwise pristine water was too deep for smaller birds.

Chuckling, Rayne imagined the forthcoming scene.

Assuredly, Fitzroy would get *his* feathers ruffled as soon as he spied the evidence the trespassing birds had left behind. A string of colorful expletives would fill the fragrant air. Especially when he noticed the disrespectful droppings currently marring Zeus's noble head and impressive shoulders.

Fitzroy would gripe and scold while suggesting several inspired ways in which to dispose of the feathered interlopers. Then he'd promptly send a younger, more agile gardener up a ladder to restore

Zeus's tattered dignity.

Rayne plucked the feathers from the fountain—a small act of kindness. She'd dispose of them near the garden's back border.

For all of Fitzroy's crotchetiness, he allowed Rayne to snip yellow roses—her favorite—and other blossoms for her bedchamber bouquets as he stood by beaming and nodding like a proud papa. On numerous occasions, he'd even pointed out which blooms were at their peak.

Grinning, Rayne clasped her dark green and peacock-blue skirts and sank into a mock curtsy before Athena, the goddess of flowers. The translucent sunbeams flickering through the branches almost made it seem as if the statue winked at her.

As Rayne had absolutely no idea about the manner in which one should address a marble deity, she simply said, "Good morning, Athena."

A grating cry rent the air, and she glanced upward.

"And good morning to you too, Theopolis," Rayne quipped to the cheeky jay that had landed upon Apollo's head and expectantly stared at her with his tiny black eyes. Shading her own eyes, she tilted her bonnetless head, her unbound hair swinging across her back and shoulders. "Isn't it a lovely day?"

The bird made a soft but shrill sound.

"Patience, Theopolis."

In truth, she didn't know if the bird were male or female. Or, in fact, if it was the same flirtatious bird that greeted her nearly every morning. The pinkish-brown jay with its distinctive blue-and-black striped wing markings dipped its little head as if in agreement, waiting for the bread scraps she often brought with her.

She reasoned it must be the same bird since it made a habit of greeting her. And she decided, basing her assumption on the human species, only a male would flirt so brazenly in hopes of getting a reward.

Reaching into her basket, Rayne located the stale bread and cinnamon bun she'd found in the kitchens when she'd pilfered a bite to eat for herself this morning. Nothing fancy, but enough to keep her stomach from growling as she read and sketched the morning away: a couple of rolls, a piece of yellow cheese, grapes, an apple, a jar of lemonade, and ginger biscuits.

Her purloined stash might very well last her until tea this afternoon.

"Here you are, Theopolis."

She tossed a piece of dried crust onto the ground.

With a strident cry, the jay swooped down, snatched the treat with his beak, and flew away. In his wake, a clouded yellow butterfly drifted toward the periwinkle colored scabious, no doubt to enjoy sweet nectar for breakfast.

Rayne made a mental note to try to sketch the next clouded yellow she saw feeding. Doing so would test her artistic abilities, but she enjoyed challenging herself. Shouldn't one want to continually improve in some small way?

Spinning in a small circle, she sighed contentedly.

This was simply lovely.

Summer was her favorite season and morning her preferred time of day.

She'd awoken early, as was her custom, despite not having sought her bed until well past midnight. The ball hosted by her Aunt Everleigh and her husband, Griffin Dalton, Duke of Sheffield, last night had been a veritable crush and, therefore, a roaring *haut ton* success.

At least three hundred of *le beau monde's* finest had attended, ensuring write-ups in all of the gossip rags and newssheets that were of any account. Yes, the ball had been a rousing triumph.

And made more so because her dear friend, Nicolette Twistleton, had received a very romantic, very sigh-worthy public marriage proposal from Mathias Pembroke, Duke of Westfall. To Rayne's utter delight, Nicolette, who'd been previously jilted and had sworn off all men, had said yes.

Now Rayne and their other closest mutual friends were excited to congratulate Nicolette again and to hear all of the delicious details over several cups of steaming tea while nibbling decadent dainties, cakes, pastries, and biscuits.

Rayne was a debutante this Season—albeit a rather older debutante. She had danced several times and enjoyed a few splendid hours with her friends. Though in general, large gatherings inevitably strained her nerves.

A long-ago, disquieting memory tried to impose itself upon her current happiness. Rayne wasn't having any of that today. Purposefully tamping down the unpleasant recollection, she unceremoniously shoved the unsolicited remembrance into a distant corner as she'd learned to do over the years.

Nothing would ruin this delightful morning.

Today no heavy haze of coal dust layered the city, and the air was fairly fresh for London. The sky shone vivid blue for a change, with only a few wispy clouds feathered across the far horizon. Several birds' calls echoed from the trees and shrubberies in Griffin's illustrious grounds and also the less formal gardens next door.

Resuming her song, Rayne continued on the meandering footpath, each footfall a satisfyingly crisp *crunch* on the gravel.

"In June there was a yellow rosebud..."

Headed toward the farthest corner of the garden, she touched a fingertip to a velvety sun-colored rose as she passed by. On that side of the grounds, a stone wall, inlaid with small, projecting steps on both sides, separated the Sheffields' gardens from their neighbors'.

Neighbors who hadn't been in residence in a very long while, according to Griffin. Since before he'd purchased this stately house, in fact. And neighbors who, at one time, must've been close friends with whoever had owned the manor before Griffin.

For why else would the stairs permit easy access across the wall if that were not the case? Perchance the residents of the two households had been relatives. She would have to remember to ask Griffin about that.

Mayhap he knew the history of the empty house and its owners. Or perhaps he knew if and when they were expected to return to London. In the meanwhile, Rayne fully intended to continue enjoying the cozy fairy-like garden with its utterly delightful stacked-stone folly.

Did Griffin or Everleigh know about the steps in the wall?

Probably not, and she wasn't positive that she wanted to share her secret. After all, Rayne was the one who enjoyed exploring every enchanting nook and cranny, just as she had at Fittledale Park.

A small stab of nostalgia speared her, and she tightened her mouth for a pace.

She missed Fittledale Park, the quiet country estate near Colchester that Everleigh had purchased after her first husband's death. In point of fact, Rayne found nearly everything about London overwhelming: the routs, balls, soirees, musicals, the theater...*the men.*

Mostly the men.

She'd never completely outgrown her fear of males and, truth be told, doubted she ever would.

Although outings to Hyde Park, Green Park, and St. James' Park were enjoyable, one never knew how many acquaintances one might encounter. And worse, be forced to discuss trivial drivel with them. Unless she were atop a horse. On those occasions, Rayne could gallop Rotten Row and not have to partake in the usual boring twaddle.

And then there were the never-ending assemblies...

Well, honestly. They were nothing short of a perpetual competition to see who was the first tulip of fashion; who would dance with whom; who might make a brilliant match this Season; whom might give someone the cut; and what succulent gossip might be spread about with the ease of whipped butter on a fresh-from-the-oven hot cross bun.

Rayne peered ahead to where the path ended near a pink tea rose-smothered arbor set before a stunning octagon cobalt-blue, sea-green, lavender, and white tile mosaic. An ostentatious sundial in the mosaic's center commanded one's attention, much like a grand dame entering a salon or prima donna upon the stage.

Impressive and impossible to ignore.

Her musings returned to the mysterious stairs. Surely Fitzroy, if no one else, must be aware of the unusual wall separating the properties. If Griffin didn't know the wall's history, mayhap the gardener did.

Fitzroy had come with the manor. Griffin had often said, "I don't think there is any question of him retiring to the country."

The charming rock expanse ran parallel to a tall,

well-maintained hedgerow. So conceivably, the gardener hadn't given it much thought. There wasn't much reason to because no one occupied 19 Belford Square—the house next door.

That was rather unfortunate since the place was quite charming, in a lonely sort of way. As if it pined for its owners to return and fill it with life and love once more.

Nevertheless, the slightly overgrown gardens were something to behold. Whoever had designed them had possessed quite the artistic eye.

As meticulous and attractive as Fitzroy kept the Sheffields' grounds, the unkempt, natural beauty of the property next door beckoned Rayne as it had since she'd accidentally discovered it when she'd come to live in London after Aunt Everleigh had married Griffin.

In truth, Everleigh wasn't really Rayne's aunt.

Well, she was her step-aunt by marriage, but they shared no blood.

Such trivialities didn't matter to either of them. The women had grown as close as sisters while

Everleigh had been married to Rayne's grand-uncle, Arnold Chatterton. Arnold had been estranged from his sister for many years and was a stranger to Rayne. Nevertheless, Grandmother's brother had been appointed her guardian when Mama and Grandma had died from influenza within a week of one another.

Now there had been an evil, *evil* man, as had been his equally depraved son, Frederick. Both spawns of Satan now likely—*and deservedly*—warmed hell's deepest bowels.

A shiver scuttled down Rayne's spine and lifted the flesh along her arms. Her earlier joy evaporated with the alacrity of a water droplet sprinkled upon a roaring fire, taking her cheerful smile with it.

How very different Griffin was from Arnold and Frederick, thank God.

Even so, Rayne didn't doubt memories yet haunted Everleigh as much as they did her from the time they'd spent under Arnold and Frederick Chatterton's cruel thumbs. At thirteen, Rayne had gone to live at Keighsdon Hall and had endured their vindictiveness several years longer than Everleigh.

It had been a tumultuous, terrifying existence.

With a determined shake of her head, Rayne pushed those morose musings away and focused on the present.

Everleigh and Griffin intended to visit his lace and textile manufacturing plants today, which meant she had hours to enjoy herself in the wild tangle next door. If all went well, she'd be home—her hair properly piled atop her head in the manner of every respectable young miss on the Marriage Mart—and possessing sketches that she might later create watercolors from, well before they returned.

As she reached the stone barrier, she took up her song once more.

"In June there was a yellow rosebud..."

Singing beneath her breath, she balanced her basket atop the wall's slightly rounded top. Once she'd gathered her skirts in one hand, she ascended the narrow steps, using the wall for balance. After carefully turning around, she descended the other side.

"And that is the flow'r for me."

"And that is...hmm, hmm, hmm."

Still humming, she'd hopped onto the slightly damp, shaded ground. Angling her face upward, she shook her hair so that it tumbled down her back.

I should've at least tied it back with a ribbon.

Oh well. Too late now.

Her mind already moving to the pleasant mission she'd set herself, Rayne collected her basket. Today she meant to draw the glorious wisteria—a task that would strain her humble artistic talents. She didn't draw for praise or recognition. No, she sketched because she enjoyed trying to capture moments in time.

Everything she knew about drawing and painting had been self-taught, mostly while living at Keighsdon Hall. She had to do something with her time. Lonely, neglected, and an obvious inconvenience—Uncle Arnold hadn't even bothered with a governess after she'd turned fifteen—Rayne had learned to entertain herself.

The wisteria vine had escaped its staid arbor's confines and had twisted and entwined itself up a plane tree, creating an enchanting, fairly-like effect. The usually unremarkable tree appeared to be festooned with streaming purple flowers.

The result was quite stunning. Almost magical.

No properly attended garden would ever be permitted something so unrestrained and beautiful. A shame, really.

Why must everything be constrained by someone else's strictures and dictates of appropriateness, acceptability, or propriety?

Wasn't there any room for originality and uniqueness?

No. That was the unfortunate, undeniable if somewhat unpleasant truth.

With a slight shrug for what she was powerless to change, Rayne took up singing where'd she left off.

"I oftentimes have pluck'd that yellow rosebud..."

"Wasna it a red rosebud?" an amused male inquired in a deep, melodious brogue.

2

Shrieking, Rayne spun around and clutched the basket to her chest, certain her hammering heart was about to break through her breastbone.

Searching the shadows cast by the abundant overgrown trees and unattended shrubberies, her frantic gaze landed on a tall—*very tall*—figure several feet away. Her pulse ran rampant, scrambling through her veins as surprise and shock momentarily rendered her mute.

Good Lord.

The brute had frightened the starch out of her, ambushing her reactions and her tongue. A tidal wave of unmitigated alarm engulfed her. Why, her knees actually trembled, so startled was she. Summoning her shaken composure, she attempted to look unaffected and not like a guilty trespasser caught completely off-guard.

Which, in point of fact, was precisely what she was.

"Yes, but I prefer yellow roses," she managed, her voice quivering.

Why must songs always be about red roses?

Not everyone fancied that passionate shade.

And why in God's holy name was her mind rambling on about such nonsensical claptrap when an enormous man with shoulder-length hair as black as a moonless midnight stood with one knee bent, his big hands splayed on lean buckskin-clad hips, and calmly regarded her.

"Och."

A single syllable. Nothing more.

At her continued gaping, his lips slowly tipped up wolfishly. That was the only way to describe the upturned, confident, predatory sweep of his mouth. He was, she had to admit despite her discomfit, quite the most perfect display of masculinity she'd ever seen.

Most perfect indeed.

Her usual trepidation at seeing any man in a state of partial dishabille escaped her.

Black hair covered this man's muscled forearms, exposed by shirtsleeves rolled to his elbows. His shirt was unbuttoned halfway down his chest, revealing a tantalizing peek of more crisp raven hair. Indeed, he looked every bit as beautiful and feral as the grounds surrounding them. These gardens provided a perfect backdrop for his rugged, untamed appearance.

Who was he?

Why was he here?

Perhaps he was a newly hired gardener. In which case, that meant someone was likely taking up residence, and her surreptitious forays to this secret hideaway must cease.

Her heart plunked to her shoes, where it wallowed in abject disappointment and self-pity.

Rayne scarcely had a moment to contemplate this most unsatisfactory turn of events before the man—Scots she presumed from his lyrical accent—prowled toward her. And even though her heart thumped as frantically as a caged bird behind her ribs and her mouth had gone as dry as the stale bread she'd tossed Theopolis, she couldn't help but notice the stranger's sleek, sinewy, male grace as he advanced.

This was no dandified lord who padded his garments.

Oh, God.

Mayhap he wasn't a gardener after all but a vagrant.

Or a criminal.

Or...or worse.

She swallowed against another surge of dread. She despised being timid and fearful—a quaking, quivering little mouse.

Squinting, she tried to make out his features.

Unfortunately, she was looking into the sun, and a very annoying sunbeam seemed determined to shine directly in her eyes.

Had he noticed the house was vacant and taken it upon himself to dwell there?

She'd heard of the many homeless people inhabiting London, but to brazenly move into a house in this elite neighborhood was certain to garner attention.

From beneath her eyelashes, she examined him.

No. Not a vagabond.

Though midnight bristle covered his granite jaw, he wasn't filthy, nor were his clothes disheveled in the manner of the beggars she'd seen on rare occasions. Dirt did cling to his expensive boots, and a long, irregular smudge across his torso marred the white of his fine lawn shirt. Regardless, even across the distance, she recognized the quality of his attire.

A breeze whispered past, cooling her flushed face. The sun sifted through the lacy entanglement of the overgrown trees overhead, casting his chiseled face in contrasting shadow and light—light and shadow.

Equally sinister and stunning. Intriguing and chilling.

He looked familiar, but Rayne couldn't quite place him. It was possible she'd met him at one of the various functions Everleigh had towed her to these past months.

If only the sunlight and shadows weren't playing

tricks with his arresting face and her vision. Rayne pulled the inner corners of her eyebrows together in concentration.

Where had she seen him?

Not… *Sweet Jesus. No!*

Her stomach sank sickeningly as her heart hammered with the power of a brawny blacksmith striking an anvil behind her ribcage.

Please, *please* not at Keighsdon Hall—her former guardian's home.

Bile billowed, burning an acrid trail up her too-tight throat.

Swallowing with difficulty, she adjusted her stance for a swift flight. Except, she instinctively knew, this wasn't a man she could easily escape. Trepidation turned her blood cold, and sweat dampened her palms and beneath her arms.

Stupid, stupid, stupid.

Why hadn't she turned tail and run the instant he'd spoken?

Rayne could have been safely within the confines of Griffin's manor by now.

Had this Scot been one of Uncle Arnold's *guests* at one of his debauched gatherings of the most depraved and dissolute lechers and reprobates? Was *that* where she'd seen this man previously?

If so, the danger had just multiplied exponentially.

Genuine panic sluiced through Rayne now. Her fingertips had turned to ice, and her stomach quivered from apprehension.

Could she manage the wall's little stairs before he was upon her?

Would anyone hear her if she screamed?

Had Griffin and Everleigh departed yet?

Where was Fitzroy?

The other gardeners?

Questions buzzed around inside her head, a confusing cacophony, like a swarm of agitated bees protecting their hive.

Blast it all.

This was Thursday, which meant the gardeners were tending the front beds. Regular as clockwork— front beds Mondays and Thursdays. As if there was a single blade of grass brazen enough to peek higher than the precise two inches Fitzroy allowed the lush, verdant carpet.

What was she to do?

Rayne retreated until her back scraped against the rough, cold stone. Thrusting her basket straight out in front of her—a pathetic, inadequate shield—she attempted to ward the stranger off.

"S...stay where y...you are. C...come no f...further."

She loathed that her voice trembled, and her hands shook so badly that the basket's contents rattled like brass buttons in a tin. Truth be told, bravery and courage were not characteristics she possessed in abundance. However, she didn't typically stammer and trip over her tongue either.

Halting a mere ten feet away, the stranger chuckled and gave the quaking basket a pointed glance. The blasted capricious sun was doing its bloody utmost to blind her and made it impossible to see him clearly.

Yet again, recognition tapped the recesses of Rayne's mind.

She *had* seen him before.

Who *was* he?

One hand clasped at the back of his neck, he dipped his head. The movement pulled his shirt taut across sculpted muscles and brought his face into sharp focus. The sun's glow cast an iridescent aura around him. He smiled, almost boyishly, revealing a row of even, white teeth.

Of course, he had perfect teeth. The man was practically a Greek god in human form. He put the statues in Griffin's gardens to shame.

Of its own volition, her attention sank to his groin.

Was he better endowed *there* than those marble deities as well? She'd always thought their *appendages* rather inadequate for immortals.

Fire heated her cheeks at her wanton musings, and her focus flew back to his face.

Had he noticed her intimate, highly improper perusal?

Lord.

Rayne almost groaned aloud. Caught ogling a man's private bits, as brazen as a ladybird or light-skirt. What in God's precious name had come over her?

A ghost of a smile twitched his mouth the tiniest bit at the corners. Fine lines bracketed those lips and pleated the edges of his eyes as if he smiled often.

He possessed quite a nice mouth.

Probably the pleasantest she'd ever seen on a man.

Nicely shaped, the lips evenly plump—not too thick or thin. The dark stubble covering his jaw reminded her of the swashbuckler she'd read about in one of the romance novels Nicolette Twistleton had secretly given her to read.

To be perfectly honest, dressed as he was, his longish hair shifting as the wind caught it, all he needed was a dashing crimson sash tied at his trim waist, a gold hoop earring, and a large sword to complete his buccaneer persona.

Rayne canted her head, considering him.

Mayhap a black hat with a vibrant purple ostrich feather or two as well.

Have you completely lost your mind, Rayne Evie Leona Wellbrook?

Once more, her stomach toppled over itself when he shook his head, tossing his hair back, and she realized he did indeed have a small gold band hanging from his left ear. As if reading her thoughts, he curved that strong mouth into a full, unfettered smile, transforming him from menacing to breathtakingly beautiful.

Rayne forgot to breathe, and her jaw nearly went slack at the unexpected change in his appearance.

She recognized his kind—confident, carefree scoundrels. Rakehells of the worst sort. Roués and rapscallions. Smoldering temptation fairly oozed off him, and she grudgingly accepted her frenetic heartbeat and hot face mightn't be blamed entirely on fright.

That unwelcome knowledge shook Rayne to her core. Never before had she experienced this immediate attraction to a man.

In fact, the opposite was generally true. Men—strangers—usually frightened her.

"I dinna think yer wee basket is a verra effective means of protectin' ye, lass."

Definitely Scottish.

Humor dripped from each word, his melodic burr rolling over her like a vocal caress. *That voice*. It did all sorts of unexpected things to her joints, thoughts, and pulse.

He chuckled and, perversely irked, she came back to herself in a rush.

Why, the uncouth brute *was* laughing at her.

Rayne snatched the useless basket to her chest, and after fumbling beneath the cloth covering the food, her book, and the sketching materials, she found what she sought.

"No, but *this* is."

She whipped out the small paring knife she'd intended to use to peel her apple.

Throwing his head back and exposing the thick column of his sun-browned throat, he laughed heartily. Shoulders shaking and hilarity shining in his eyes— striking blue-green eyes the likes of which she'd never seen before—he shook his head. His slightly wavy hair gleamed blue-black where the sun kissed it.

Marine-colored beams roved over her, steady and

assessing.

Why was she noticing any of this?

Her virtue—her life—might very well be in peril.

"Lass, ye dinna mean to stab me with *that* wee thing?"

3

With considerable effort, Fletcher wrestled his mirth under control. The lovely English rose presently threatening to skewer him obviously didn't appreciate his laughing at her expense.

Damn, but she was an unexpected, refreshing delight.

When he'd ventured into the gardens two hours ago to tackle some of the unmanageable shrubberies and, more on point, to work off some of the frustration his mother's endless meddling had caused, his manservant and friend, Leith MacKettrick, had raised his skeptical, grizzled coppery brows.

"Ye dinna mean to tend the grounds yerself, Fletcher?" Leith had asked with a dubious wrinkling of his forehead and downward slant of his mouth.

"Nae, only until ye see to hirin' the staff." Fletcher slapped Leith on his broad shoulder. "Ye ken, I prefer the outdoors and bein' active. Two months of livin' like a dandified London sot has me as fidgety as a panther in a too-small cage."

At this very moment, Leith was putting notices at the various agencies and registrar offices for a cook, two maids of all work, a footman-butler, and a groundskeeper. As Fletcher meant to leave London soon, there wasn't a need to fully staff the house. Those few servants would suffice just fine until he departed.

He congratulated himself on his good fortune that this property had just become available and that it was a goodly distance from his mother's residence. It was also fortunate that he wasn't a man who minded getting his hands dirty. He and Leith had spent the early morning hours removing Holland cloths and rearranging furniture to his satisfaction.

A throaty contralto had originally alerted him to his unexpected visitor.

THE DEBUTANTE AND THE DUKE

His first sight of this spitfire had been a delightfully turned ankle and trim, pale blue stocking-clad calf swinging over the wall. Naturally, as any tenant worth his salt would do, he'd watched the brazen intruder with avid attention. That well-shaped leg had turned into an even lovelier plump bottom. When she'd wriggled back and forth as she shimmied onto the top stair, his groin had pulled with carnal male appreciation.

At present, color flagging her high cheekbones, her amber-brown eyes flashing gold sparks, and her gorgeous gold-and-bronze-threaded sable hair tumbling around her shoulders and down her back, she looked like a startled garden nymph caught popping uninvited into his grounds.

He glanced downward, half-expecting to find bare feet peeking from beneath the hem of her gown.

Nae, pink toes.

Just sensible black half boots he'd seen earlier as she gracefully scaled the wall with an efficiency that suggested she'd done so many times before.

A most intriguing and peculiarly welcome discovery.

From beneath half-closed eyelids, Fletcher took in her gown and the lusciously rounded curves that the quality fabric gave a tantalizing hint of. Garden nymphs didn't wear expensive marine-colored gowns either.

Her fierce, determined expression as she wielded the tiny blade caused a surge of admiration. Most Englishwomen would've had a fit of histrionics or the vapors upon being so startled. At least, most of the ones he was acquainted with would've done. None would've dared exit a house without gloves and a bonnet either, as this spitfire had.

Instead, this trespassing little minx with her unbound hair acted as if *he* were the intruder.

Fletcher had a fairly good notion of who she was—his neighbor, the Duke of Sheffield's niece by marriage, Rayne Wellbrook. He'd seen her at numerous *ton* events since he'd arrived in London last April, although they'd never been formally introduced.

In general, he kept well clear of unmarried English misses, particularly innocent debutantes. They all had one thing on their minds. *Marriage*. No, make that two things—marriage and marrying well, which meant snaring a coveted title.

Fletcher wasn't opposed to marriage per se—just marriage to a pampered and cossetted Englishwoman. As he was half-English himself, the hypocrisy of his aversion didn't escape him.

Hopefully, he'd wrap up his business dealings soon and could return to Dumfries in short order. His mother strenuously objected, of course, preferring he remain in London at her beck and call.

So she can bleed more funds from me.

Rather insincere for a woman who had abandoned her husband and children to return to her native England and take up with her equally discontented and spoiled cohorts.

Mother justified her desertion by vowing her gently-bred constitution was too delicate and the Scots too uncivilized for her to remain in Scotland any longer.

Greg, four years Fletcher's junior, had cried for weeks. Then one day, he simply stopped grieving, and the cheerful little boy he'd been had disappeared as well. Now, at nearly six-and-twenty, he seldom smiled, let alone laughed. He'd become jaded, cold, and somber.

Fletcher's parents' union had been an arranged marriage of convenience. After a dozen years of constant complaining, Mother had flown the nest. She'd provided the heir and spare, and her duty was complete. Or so she declared with cold disdain that day she'd climbed into the coach and hadn't looked back.

That had been eighteen years ago.

In point of fact, Father hadn't been positive that Florence was his daughter, but Mother had left the almost one-year-old infant behind, nonetheless. At one-and-thirty, Fletcher's mother had been determined to enjoy the lifestyle her status afforded her and indulge in all the things she had missed by marrying straight out of the schoolroom, a man two-and-twenty years her senior.

Now nearing fifty and still quite beautiful, Rosalind, Duchess of Kincade, was known far and wide for her flamboyant lifestyle, her many, *many* younger lovers, her penchant for gambling and drinking champagne, and her ridiculous obsession with shoes and bonnets.

The last milliner's bill had Fletcher gnashing his teeth.

Bloody hell.

How many damned shoes or bonnets did one woman need?

Mother had been none too pleased when he'd informed her last week that if she overspent her allowance in the future, he'd not pay her creditors. Her whining and theatrics had affected Fletcher not at all except to reaffirm his resolve to depart her company at the earliest convenience.

After two months of her hospitality, petulant pouts, manipulations, and machinations to wed him to a *proper English* chit, he'd been determined to obtain his own residence in any event.

Or take to the bottle as his daffy, brokenhearted father had.

It was most opportune that not only was Sheffield one of his business partners, but the fellow also had knowledge of an empty house in a respectable neighborhood Fletcher could move into straightaway.

And so here he was. Letting 19 Bedford Square, of all places. Like a bloody damned proper English duke, to boot.

Only, Fletcher was a Scottish duke and didn't give ten shillings what *le beau monde* thought of him. He'd never sought the favor of English peers. He conceded, amongst the *ton's* upper ten thousand, there were several decent chaps, including Sheffield, the dukes of San Sebastian and Asherford, as well as a half dozen or so others. There were also a great number of absolute, unmitigated asslings.

His new accommodations were in need of a good clean and the grounds a bit of rigorous attention, but all in all, for a Sassenach residence, it was quite pleasant. He especially liked the untamed gardens. They reminded him of Levensyde House, his home a couple of miles outside of Dumfries.

Fletcher had considered letting rooms at one of his clubs, but his brother and sister might want to stay in London at some point. Florence longed for a proper Come Out and a Season in London. Something his grasping mother fully supported, naturally.

Mother would likely try to insist Florence reside with her, though she knew her own daughter not at all. No doubt the conniving duchess already had some randy decrepitude in mind for his sweet sister as well. All to advance Mother's social standing and circle of influence, of course.

The idea made him shudder. Florence was too sweet and innocent for London.

Dragging his thoughts from his unpleasant ruminations to the very pleasant creature before him, Fletcher offered her a friendly grin, intending to lessen Miss Wellbrook's unease.

"Allow me to introduce myself," he said, bending at the waist into an exaggerated formal bow he'd never before had cause to use, with one hand across his middle and the other flung wide like a courtier.

He knew full well it wasn't done. No one introduced themselves. They must go through all of the falderol and balderdash of asking a mutual acquaintance to do the honors.

Asinine and inconvenient when he wanted to

speak with this imp now.

"Fletcher McQuinton, Duke of Kincade," he informed her, only half-mockingly instead of his usual full-on jeer.

Her leery expression didn't fluctuate, nor did she so much as blink. She continued to regard him like a skittish doe prepared to bolt at the slightest hint of danger.

This was very telling indeed.

An unwed young woman who didn't turn into a simpering, pretentious numpty immediately upon learning he possessed a title, and a dukedom no less. Dukes were just this side of royalty, and Fletcher knew all too well the fawning and toadying that accompanied most introductions to a duke.

So accustomed to deflecting unwanted attention, at her unexpected lack of response, he almost let his guard down. *Almost.*

"I'm acquainted with Sheffield." He sought to reassure her while shifting his regard for a second over her head in her house's general direction. "In fact," he said with another genial smile, "we are in business together. I also put in an appearance at last night's ball."

A very short appearance.

Which was Fletcher's habit.

Never dally at any *haut ton* function long enough for politesse to trap him into conversing or otherwise engaging with those on the prowl for a husband. When he chose a wife, she'd be a hearty and hale, wide-hipped, sturdy Scottish lass with red cheeks and a robust constitution. A sensible woman who knew full well what hardships to expect as a Scottish duke's wife.

At last, a bit of the suspicion and tension eased from Miss Wellbrook's refined features, and she partially lowered the inadequate blade. Forehead furrowed in neat little lines, she cocked her head, taking his measure. Her expression cleared, and her berry-red, kissable rosebud lips swept upward at the edges in a closed-mouth smile.

"Ah, yes. I recognize you now, Your Grace." Her inquisitive, coppery brown-eyed gaze took in his loose hair. "Your hair was pulled back into a queue."

4

Indeed, it was.

There was neither approval nor disapproval in Miss Wellbrook's voice at Fletcher's unfashionable choice. He refused to grow side whiskers or wear his hair in the popular dandified styles: Brutus, Caesar, Titus, or the frightened owl.

Who in God's name wanted to go about looking like a bloody terrified fowl had gone to battle with one's hair? A fop or a dandy who gave more than two damns about his appearance, Fletcher would never be—to his mother's utter and complete vexation.

All the more reason to refuse to abide by society's strictures.

"And you escorted Lady Sheldon-Furnsby." Miss

Wellbrook's tone took on a cooler and far less neutral edge.

That, too, was most telling.

Lady Cecelia Sheldon-Furnsby's tenacious, hell-cat reputation preceded her, it would seem. And by God, not a word about her unpleasant character was a bloody exaggeration.

The woman had sought him out as aggressively and doggedly as a crazed hound on the fresh scent of a fox. Ever determined, she'd cornered Fletcher last evening and latched onto his arm, much like a tick on a dog or a barnacle on a ship's hull. Each required considerable effort and resolve to dislodge.

As had Lady Sheldon-Furnsby last night.

He'd only managed to pry her talons off when he'd pled a fabricated need to use the necessary to relieve himself.

She'd offered to accompany him and *help*.

Brazen as a dockside strumpet.

Fletcher hadn't a doubt last evening's unpleasant encounter with her ladyship was more of his mother's high-handed interference. Lady Cecelia Sheldon-

Furnsby was a wealthy widow.

"She's a blueblood, Kincade, descended from centuries of bluebloods. Her breeding is impeccable." Mother's strident invections yet rang in his ears. "She is *everything* one could want in a duchess."

Everything his mother wanted in a duchess.

Cecelia's flawless lineage was all that the current Duchess of Kincade cared about.

The fact that if Cecelia didn't bear a title, she'd be labeled a mean-tempered whore didn't faze Dear Mama. Cecelia made the Biblical Jezebel look like an innocent, fresh-faced milkmaid.

However, *her* mother just happened to be *his* mother's closest confidant for most of their adult lives—just under two-and-thirty years. Those two conspirators had plotted a union between him and Cecelia since they'd both been in leading strings.

To the ladies' meddling chagrin, Cecelia had married another, much older lord of the realm five years ago when Fletcher had made it quite clear he wasn't taking a woman of the same ilk as his mother to wife. He'd seen firsthand what kind of misery a mismatch like that caused, and he wasn't having any of it.

Now that she was out of mourning—*damn my eyes*—it would appear Lady Sheldon-Furnsby had set her sparkling cap for him.

She was going to be highly disappointed again.

As was Mother.

Eventually, Fletcher would marry, and when he did, it would be to a woman who hadn't a qualm about *rusticating and moldering away* in Scotland, as his mother put it.

When his uninvited garden guest still did not offer to introduce herself but, instead, bit her lip and peered longingly over his shoulder at the moss-covered folly, he said, "And ye are Miss Rayne Wellbrook."

Her light brown, bronze-tinged eyes wide, Rayne swung him a disconcerted glance.

"I am. How did you know?" Brushing that glorious hair off her shoulder, she gave him a self-conscious smile. "That was a silly question. I suppose Griffin told you."

She dropped the knife into her basket with a little

clink.

Evidently, she'd decided Fletcher posed no immediate threat to her wellbeing.

Nodding, he angled sideways, giving her an unobstructed view of the gardens behind him. "I've let this property for at least the duration of my time in London." He swept his contented gaze over the area. "I may decide to purchase the place. My sister would like a London Season."

"Oh." There was no mistaking the disappointment shadowing Rayne's pretty features.

He dropped his gaze to her basket. "I gather ye come here often?"

"Umm, yes." Pink tinging her cheeks, she fiddled with the basket's handle. "It's very peaceful. I like to read and sketch here. It doesn't feel like I'm in the middle of a large city. Griffin's gardens are quite lovely, but I find these much more relaxing. What's more, I don't have to worry about appearances here."

She gestured to her shimmering hair.

A woman who preferred these neglected grounds to Sheffield's fervently attended ones?

Enchanting and no' a little attractive.

Despite himself and the discordant warning bells clanging in his head, Fletcher became even more fascinated.

"Rayne is an unusual name." If he recollected correctly, there was a place in Aberdeenshire called Rayne.

"It means song. My mother was an opera singer. Well, she was until she married Papa. She said music was a balm to the soul."

A lovely name for a lovely lass with a lovely voice.

Fletcher almost winced at the rather appalling poetic codswallop mincing through his mind.

Another charming flush stole up her creamy cheeks as if she'd realized how much she'd revealed to a perfect stranger. "I beg your pardon for intruding."

She turned and placed her basket on the rounded ledge, then gathered her skirts. Bracing her other palm upon the stones, she stepped onto the narrow foothold.

"I dinna mind if ye stay and sketch, lass."

Why the hell had he blurted that?

Of course, she couldn't stay.

She was unmarried, and they had no chaperone.

Nae one will ken. Och, someone will see and say somethin'.

Things like that always had a way of leaking out, no matter how discrete one attempted to be. Aye, it was much wiser all the way around for Rayne Wellbrook to leave. Promptly.

Fletcher didn't need or want any entanglements or complications. Nor did he relish infuriating the Duke of Sheffield. He valued the man's friendship every bit as much as he needed him as a business partner and investor.

Rayne's focus veered to the folly once more, and she caught the corner of her mouth between her teeth.

Was that where she'd intended to spend the morning?

The moment lengthened, stretching out, and he held his breath. His stomach muscles tightened in anticipation of her answer. She flexed her fingertips on the stone, the neat round oval of her nails digging into the uneven surface, her indecision a tangible thing.

After another half a dozen heartbeats, she finally

gave a little reluctant shake of her head. Her long hair swirled around her shoulders.

Could those tresses possibly be as silky as they looked?

Warm chocolate or impossibly soft velvet?

"No. It wouldn't be seemly. But I do thank you for the generous offer, Your Grace."

Generous, my ass.

He simply wanted to get to know this astonishing woman better.

Danger, danger, danger, chimed his exasperating and intrusive conscience.

Go to hell, he thought mutinously.

"I'll stand here to make sure ye dinna fall." Fletcher might've let her exit through the kitchen door, but the truth was that he hoped to see another delectable length of female leg.

Ye're a rotter through and through, Fletcher Anthony Patrick McQuinton.

Aye, he was, because he didn't even blink so as not to miss a single moment of the shapely spectacle.

Hitching her knee over the top of the wall, she

chuckled, a lyrical husky sound that sent awareness of her as a woman winging through his veins.

"I assure you, I've done this many times."

Just as he'd suspected.

"I shan't fall." She finished climbing over the top. "Good day, Your Grace."

A nascent smile curving those ripe lips, she collected her basket and disappeared.

Arms folded and feeling oddly discontent and put out, Fletcher remained staring at the spot he'd last seen her bronze-tinged sable hair.

What a captivating creature.

She's nae for ye. She's English. A Sassenach.

English roses such as Rayne Wellbrook wilt and die in Scotland.

Her face appeared over the wall's rounded top, and he couldn't stop the grin spreading across his face.

"Forget somethin', lass?

"Yes." A small furrow appeared at the bridge of her nose. "Please forgive me for taking it upon myself to make use of the gardens, Your Grace. It won't happen again. I give my word."

Too bad, that.

She appeared adorably flustered as she met his gaze before she dropped her attention to her hands, gripping the top of the wall. "I'd…uh…would very much appreciate it if you…uh…kept this between us."

Och, so Sheffield and his duchess didn't know about Miss Wellbrook's clandestine horticultural excursions onto Fletcher's grounds. Well, his for the time being, that was.

He flexed his shoulders in a casual shrug.

"Nae one was usin' the gardens. I canna find fault in ye enjoyin' them." He winked and was immediately rewarded by another pretty blush. "Yer welcome to visit anytime, Miss Wellbrook. Just send a note around, and one of my staff will let ye in through the kitchen door."

A narrow, cobbled alley ran between the two grand houses where deliveries were made to the kitchens and which also led to the mews behind the manors. She should be able to enter and exit without notice, thereby alleviating tongue wagging.

"I don't think that would be wise." She thinned

her ruby lips into a flat ribbon. "Even the most loyal of servants gossip on occasion."

"Ye may bring yer maid and a footman if ye wish to appear perfectly proper."

Why was he so bloody persistent?

Just let her go.

No good could come of his fascination with the wood nymph.

"Rayne? *Rayne*?" The duchess's dulcet tones filtered through the greenery. "Are you out here, dear?"

"Bother. I thought they'd left already," Rayne whispered.

She put her forefinger to her lips, drawing Fletcher's attention once more to their plump redness. Had she eaten berries for breakfast?

Would her mouth still taste of their sweetness?

Her big brown doe eyes begged him to remain silent and not give her away.

"Oh, look," she breathed, pointing toward the pale blue butterfly hovering near a tree branch shading the wall. She cast him a delighted smile, and his heart skipped a couple of beats.

"It's a holly blue," she said. "I've never seen one in the city before, although they are known to frequent town gardens."

Fletcher stepped onto the lowest step. Balancing on the small protrusion with ease, he murmured low into her ear, "Promise ye'll visit again, Miss Rayne Wellbrook."

Her fragrance surrounded him, a heady, enticing aroma. Gardenia and carnation and woman. Sweet and spicy and—God help him for a fool—tempting as hell.

He was a bloody damned idiot for encouraging her to come here again.

Rayne tossed a fretful glance over her shoulder, then peeked up at him through those bronze-tipped, sooty lashes. Though she was tall for a woman and stood on a step, he still claimed several inches on her.

"I mustn't come again now that you are in residence," she said, her voice barely audible. "I cannot risk ruination. We haven't even been formally introduced, Your Grace."

"Rayne?" came the duchess again, this time much

closer and with genuine concern weighting her voice.

"I shall speak with Sheffield on the matter." Fletcher lowered his head until his lips nearly brushed the graceful curves of Rayne's shell-like ear. Only half an inch to spare.

What would she do if he touched his mouth just there?

To the tantalizing, petal-soft flesh just below her earlobe?

He blew softly.

Sucking in a sharp, irregular breath, she stiffened.

He inhaled her essence, his pulse quickening with immediate arousal.

"I'm positive an introduction willna be hard to arrange, *lèannan*. I'll insist on it."

5

Hyde Park, London
Four days later in the afternoon

Feeling oddly out of sorts despite the day's temperate weather and the adorable, fluffy ducklings paddling along the Serpentine, Rayne kept pace with Everleigh, Gabriella, Duchess of Pennington, Gabriella's sister, Ophelia Breckensole, and Theadosia, Duchess of Sutcliffe.

They were to meet Jemmah, Duchess of Dandridge, and Sophronie Slater for tea at Nicolette's in just over an hour.

Normally, Rayne would've keenly anticipated that particular gathering. These were her dearest friends, after all. But since her encounter with the Duke of Kincade four days ago, she'd been peculiarly restless and oddly discontented.

Agitated even.

He'd seemed so determined she visit his gardens again and had insisted on an introduction. Almost as if he were truly interested in her. However, it appeared his grace wasn't so very enthusiastic after all, as four days had passed with nary a note nor an appearance.

Four days wasn't so very long—just over half a week, she reasoned.

Are you listening to yourself? her logical self severely scolded.

Since when did *she* desire a man's attention?

Honestly?

Since she'd stumbled upon that enigmatic Scot in her secret oasis and, after overcoming her initial shock, had realized he didn't make her feel uncomfortable or wary.

No, indeed. *That* most assuredly wasn't what the disarming Duke of Kincade made her feel at all.

His grace's last masculine purr in her ear, his

warm breath a sensual caress, had sent all of her senses tumbling pell-mell. Like a frightened mouse, she'd fled his presence without another word or a backward glance. Rayne vowed she'd heard the rich, melodious tenor of his chuckle as she skirted the hedgerow and found her way to Everleigh.

The handsome blighter.

What if Everleigh had overheard Him? Them?

She hadn't, thank the divine powers.

That would've resulted in a slew of questions Rayne would rather not answer.

As it turned out, Everleigh had received today's invitation to take tea with Nicolette and wanted to ensure Rayne made no other plans.

As if she would do so of her own accord.

Everleigh had to gently prod her at almost every turn to venture into society. While some debutantes thrived on the social whirlwind, Rayne relished a more sedate lifestyle. Her aunt was never unkind, nor did she force her if she were truly opposed to attending any function. But she fretted about Rayne's future which, in turn, caused Rayne distress.

She didn't want to be a burden to Everleigh or Griffin. But the unvarnished truth was that she was a penniless orphan, completely reliant upon the Sheffields. Uncle Albert hadn't provided a dowry or any other provision for her, and if it hadn't been for Eveleigh's kind and generous nature, Rayne wasn't certain what would've become of her when her guardian had unexpectedly died.

In point of fact, he and Frederick had been murdered. Rayne still harbored a degree of guilt for feeling no remorse or sorrow at their passings. Only blessed relief that she'd be forevermore spared their vile presence and their even more abhorrent gatherings.

"I simply want you to be as happy and content as I am, Rayne," Everleigh had said during breakfast this morning as she spread strawberry preserves on her quarter piece of toast.

How many times had Rayne heard that?

Far, far too many to count.

For at least as many times, Rayne had replied, "I know you do, and I am so very grateful."

She did know, and her heart overflowed with appreciation. Not all young women were nearly as blessed and privileged as she. Providence had smiled upon Everleigh too, and if ever a soul merited such good fortune, it was Rayne's selfless aunt.

Neither mentioned the heartbreak and misery Everleigh had suffered before Griffin came into her life at Theadosia's Christmastide house party last year. Just as neither woman mentioned why Rayne feared most men, though, through years of practice, she kept her trepidation well-disguised on the outside.

The turmoil and apprehension that beset her inwardly was another matter entirely.

This afternoon, she wore one of the many new gowns Everleigh and Griffin had insisted that, as a debutante, Rayne required for her Season. Her arguments that she was two-and-twenty and well past the age for a formal come out hadn't dissuaded either in the slightest. She'd welcomed her introduction to *le beau monde* with as much enthusiasm as having acquired a large carbuncle on her bottom or an oozing blister upon her upper lip.

The same ability that enabled her to mask her fear of men also aided her in donning a pleasant mien at social functions. Not even her closest friends knew the whole ugly truth—just bits and buttons.

None except Everleigh.

The others knew enough to understand why she behaved as she did at times.

Allowing a budding smile, Rayne ran a gloved hand over her skirt.

This ivory-and-pink-striped gown was truly lovely, and despite her qualms, she appreciated the exquisite frock. The blush-colored spencer—the exact same shade of pink as the gown's stripes—was made of the softest velvet Rayne had ever felt. Naturally, her white kid half boots, pink gloves, and silk bonnet with its plethora of pink-and-white silk flowers enhanced the ensemble.

To be perfectly frank, she felt rather like a dressed-up doll on display. This gorgeous costume drew unsolicited attention to her.

How could it not?

Of the latest style and sewn by Mademoiselle

Franciose Beauchêne, one of London's most exclusive modistes, the becoming garment was meant to be precisely what it was—a beacon of fashion. A calling card and advertisement for Mademoiselle Beauchêne.

Regardless, Rayne longed for a plain gown that she didn't have to worry about soiling or tearing. Just as she yearned for the peace and quiet of the neighboring gardens. Gardens which—most tiresomely—were now off-limits to her unless she brought a maid and a footman along.

And dragging bored servants with her defeated the very purpose in seeking a solitary place.

"You're awfully quiet today, Rayne." Gabriella peered at her from beneath the brim of a fetching yellow-and-peach bonnet. "Are you quite well?"

A small crease between her eyebrows revealed her genuine concern.

"I was thinking the same thing," Ophelia piped in as she looped her hand through Rayne's elbow. Winged eyebrows raised questioningly, she nudged Rayne gently in the ribs.

No surprise there. Gabriella and Ophelia were

twins and frequently not only voiced the same thoughts but finished each other's sentences.

"I'm perfectly fine." Rayne tilted her mouth into a bright, if somewhat forced, smile. "I've just been thinking about Nicolette." She had been—sort of. Before her mind had taken her down several rabbit trails. "I'm so very pleased for her."

A chorus of agreements echoed her declaration.

Ophelia grinned as she leaned into Rayne's shoulder. "Who do you think will be next?"

"Next?" Rayne puzzled her brow.

"Yes, goose. Next to become betrothed? Wed? Caught in the parson's mousetrap? Leg-shackled?"

Rayne lifted a shoulder as she regarded a curious jay watching them. It couldn't possibly be Theopolis. *Could it?*

"I'm sure I don't know." She did know, however, it would not be her. Unlike most women of her station, marriage had never been her end-all desire. "You don't sound as if marriage is high on your list of priorities, Ophelia."

"I haven't met the right man, I suppose," Ophelia

said a trifle too casually. "I have no wish to be a chattel or simply marry because I fear being on the shelf or growing long in the tooth."

All valid reasons Rayne commiserated with.

Nonetheless, their little troupe of unmarried friends was dwindling. In addition to those wedded ladies presently strolling the wide pathway near the Serpentine with her, Jessica Brentwood had recently made a match with Crispin Rolston, Duke of Bainbridge.

Perhaps Ophelia or Sophronie or their friend Justina Farthington would soon make a brilliant match as well. Eyeing Ophelia, Rayne teased, "Has any particular gentleman caught *your* attention?"

"*Me?*" Ophelia scoffed and elevated her chin in a rather mutinous fashion. "Certainly not. You know how restricted my life with my grandparents was in Colchester. I have no intention of relinquishing my freedom—meager though it is—to a man's dictates any time soon."

"Married life isn't *at all* restrictive if you marry for love, sister dearest." Gabriella winked naughtily, and the married women giggled.

"Indeed, it is not," Theadosia agreed, exchanging a pointed look with Everleigh, who returned her grin.

"I've found marriage to Griffin *most* satisfying," Everleigh declared, her cheeks pinkening becomingly.

That brought on another round of mirth from the trio of married duchesses.

Ophelia rolled her eyes skyward and leaned in to whisper conspiratorially to Rayne. "It seems we cannot escape their protestations of wedded bliss."

Or their not-so-veiled sexual innuendos.

Rayne knew more than most unmarried—supposedly virtuous women—did in that regard. Experience had been a harsh teacher. *For Everleigh too, but she overcame her aversion.* All-too familiar sourness stung Rayne's tongue, and she swallowed away the bitterness.

"I'm truly happy for them." She just didn't have the same yearning to marry and settle into domestic bliss, and apparently, neither did Ophelia.

"You know I am as well," her friend conceded. "But is it wrong to want something more too?"

"Not at all," Rayne said as they turned toward the entrance. A pair of laughing boys in navy-blue-and-white-striped skeleton suits raced by, their harried governess or nurse failing in her efforts to keep up with the energetic duo. "I want more too."

Rayne simply wasn't sure what that *more* was. Unlike Ophelia, who enjoyed London and all the trappings that went along with a Season, Rayne could well do without the busyness and hullabaloo of town life. She supposed that made her an oddity amongst the *ton*. Amongst most gently-bred young women as well.

Should she care about that flaw in her character?

She didn't. Not a blessed jot.

"Good afternoon, Your Graces, Miss Breckensole, Miss Wellbrook."

6

Astride a magnificent bay roan, Stanford Bancroft, the handsome, extremely tall, and severe Duke of Asherford, greeted their little troupe with a polite tip of his black felt hat.

"Asherford," Everleigh greeted warmly. "Your business with my husband must've concluded earlier than anticipated."

Was everyone conducting business with Griffin these days?

Something to do with shipping and imports and exports, and of course textiles, although no one had ever bothered informing Rayne exactly what that was. She supposed it wasn't really any of her business, but that didn't mean she wasn't curious.

At one time, members of the peerage would've balked at any involvement in commerce. And if they did dabble in trade, it was done secretly, lest they be accused of *smelling of the shop*. Times were changing, however. Wise aristocrats knew that if they didn't invest in business endeavors, all they might have left in a few years was a title and a bankrupt estate.

"Indeed." Asherford's gaze lingered on Ophelia a fraction too long to be completely acceptable.

Well, now...

Mayhap Ophelia would indeed be the next of their circle to wed, despite her protestations.

From beneath her bonnet's wide brim, Rayne slid her friend a surreptitious glance.

Was she aware of the duke's interest?

Ophelia had released Rayne's elbow and, absorbed in a loose thread on the braid of her periwinkle cuff, she seemed unaware of his perusal.

Flicking his black-gloved hand, Asherford casually gestured to the two men flanking him.

Rayne's heart took on a frantic cadence when she swept her gaze over them.

It was *him*: Fletcher McQuinton, Duke of Kincade.

He was here. In Hyde Park. Just a few feet away in all of his glorious, male splendor.

Her stomach quivered with equal parts giddiness and trepidation.

Oh, my God.

Surely he wouldn't be so bold as to request an introduction in front of her closest friends and aunt. To do so would imply a genuine interest in her.

Rayne barely resisted the impulse to let her eyelids drift shut and groan aloud.

Had she been foolish enough to do so, the moment their graces departed, the ladies would be upon her like flies on sweets, demanding to know why he'd made such a direct entreaty and why she'd reacted the way she had. Naturally, they'd read all sorts of misconceptions into his request as well as her response. And then Rayne, quite naturally, would be obliged to lie to cover the truth.

And she was a horrid—*simply horrid*—liar.

"I believe you are all acquainted with Baxter

Bathhurst, Duke of San Sebastian, and Fletcher McQuinton, Duke of Kincade," Asherford said offhandedly.

Oh, now that wrong assumption was most, *most* fortuitous indeed. The gloriously, wonderfully, wholly incorrect supposition let both Rayne and the Duke of Kincade off the proverbial hook.

Before anyone could respond, the Duke of Kincade shook his head, that unusual gold hoop in his ear glinting in the sunlight. "I'm acquainted with almost everyone," he said, flashing that bone-melting smile. "However, I've never had the pleasure of a formal introduction to Miss Wellbrook."

Drat, the disarming man.

Drat, her wobbly legs and even wobblier tummy.

He *was,* indeed, going to take advantage of the opening Asherford had unwittingly created.

"Surely that cannot be." Eveleigh's fair brows arched high on her smooth forehead as she looked between the duke and Rayne. "Why, you were at our ball four nights hence."

"I was," Kincade agreed amiably. "And I'm now

yer neighbor as well. I've let the vacant house to your right."

"That's wonderful news," Everleigh declared with her usual genial warmth. "Most convenient for all of those meetings between you and Griffin. Why now, you can simply chat across the fence."

She laughed, and the others joined in the mirth. Everyone except Rayne and Kincade, that was.

A guilty flush traced its way up Rayne's neck to her cheeks, and she studiously avoided meeting the Duke of Kincade's eyes.

Looking speculative, Everleigh put a gloved forefinger to her chin. "No, I believe a stone wall separates the properties. Doesn't it, Your Grace?"

Everleigh knew about the wall?

Biting down hard on the inside of her cheek, Rayne swung her attention between her aunt and the duke.

"Indeed, it does," the Duke of Kincade agreed.

His expression unreadable, his mannerism perfectly proper to everyone present, the duke pretended like he and Rayne had never exchanged a word. Other than the brief, polite glance in her direction, he'd not indicated any prior meeting between them.

The tension eased between her shoulder blades, enough for her to inhale a full breath again. He'd not give her away. Somehow, despite her earlier misplaced alarm, she'd known he wouldn't, and that tiny trickle of trust that had sprung up that day in the garden grew stronger.

Today the duke was clean-shaven, his strong jaw and the slight dimple in the middle of his chin on full display. As was his wont, he'd tied his hair back in what was becoming a familiar queue. His deep green riding jacket brought out the jade hues of his striking, thick-lashed eyes.

Really. Must he have such ridiculously lush lashes?

Even if she applied cosmetics to hers, they'd never compare to his.

Rayne deliberately averted her attention from his buff-covered thighs and the way the muscles bunched and flexed as he expertly controlled his stunning mount. Memories of the way his shirt had pulled taut across his chest and shoulders the other day sent a wave of most inconvenient heat pitching low in her belly.

Had she caught a fever?

This hot-cold, hot-cold business was truly becoming most annoying.

To distract herself from the peculiar sensation, she fixed her attention on his horse. Pitch-black except for a silvery-white mane and tail, the creature was perhaps the most beautiful animal she'd ever beheld.

Rayne adored horses. She had done so for as long as she could remember. Griffin had purchased a sweet-tempered mare for her, and she rode Verity along Rotten Row several times a week.

"Your gelding is magnificent, Your Grace." Relief washed through her at how normal she sounded at the deft change of subject. A small satisfied smile pulled the corners of her mouth upward the merest bit.

She'd steered the conversation away from introductions. Quite cleverly too, if she did say so herself. And she did say so, she thought rather smugly.

"Aye, Spiorad—his name means spirit in Gaelic—is an exceptional horse." A slight widening of the Duke of Kincade's smile revealed he knew precisely what pathway Rayne's thoughts had pelted down and exactly what she was up to.

Ophelia continued fussing with her ensemble, which wasn't like her at all. Once she'd dealt with the stray thread on her cuff, she turned her attention to the minuscule flecks of lint on the sleeves of her lavender spencer.

Not once did she lift her gaze above the horses' elbows or look directly at the impressive ducal trio. Quite the most peculiar thing, truth be told.

"Aye, he's a brilliant high stepper. Kincade outbid me at Tattersall's," San Sebastian, another Scot, grumbled good-naturedly.

"Kincade also outbid George Slater and the Duke of Waycross, both of whom breed horses professionally," Asherford put in with a wide grin and another long glance toward Ophelia's pert profile. "They were both quite vexed at the turn of events, I might add. Though what need they might have for a gelding, I'm not certain."

Rayne narrowed her eyes the merest bit.

Was something going on between Asherford and Ophelia?

Or was something *not* going on?

He couldn't seem to stop sending her swift little glances. And Ophelia quite intentionally, Rayne concluded, wasn't giving him the slightest notice.

"Waycross much more so when Slater's daughter bought that remarkable broodmare out from under him," San Sebastian said. "He'd been waitin' impatiently for two years for Beville to sell her so he might add the mare to his breedin' stables. He was most incensed that an *upstart American lass*—his words, no' mine—should interfere with his well-laid plans."

With a slight canting of his head, Kincade addressed Everleigh. "I regret, Your Grace, I havena been introduced to yer niece."

Why…why the crafty bounder had disregarded the talk of horseflesh and neatly brought the conversation full circle. Bold as polished brass. Directly—*the sly devil*—back to the introductions.

Rayne couldn't help but be impressed, even if she felt a trifle manipulated.

In short order, Everleigh performed the introduction. She laughed afterward. "Though I suppose, Kincade, when you join us for supper tonight, the niceties might've been conducted then."

Rayne's gaze careened to her aunt.

Supper? Tonight?

He was invited?

A ragged groan climbed up her throat, but she stifled it by biting the inside of her cheek again. She didn't know how to behave with a man she found attractive. It was a first for her, and she felt as gauche and awkward as a miss fresh from the schoolroom.

But of course, his grace would be invited.

Not only was the Duke of Kincade one of Griffin's business associates, but now he was also their neighbor at 19 Bedford Square. Rayne was aware Griffin and Everleigh had plans to entertain tonight, and she'd hoped to cry off and take a tray in her room as she often did.

It wasn't likely she'd be permitted that reprieve now.

With a forced smile, she brought her attention back to the dukes, taking care not to linger her focus too long on a certain raven-haired Scottish devil.

"I look forward to seeing all of Your Graces this evening," Everleigh said, artfully bringing an end to the conversation.

They murmured their agreements.

Botheration.

It was to be a large supper party then.

Naturally, the women present, as well as the husbands of those who were wed, would also be invited. Had Rayne really been so distracted these past few days that she'd failed to realize what Everleigh had arranged for tonight?

"Until tonight, gentlemen," Gabriella said before giving her sister a troubled glance.

Ah, she'd noticed Ophelia's preoccupation too. Thus far, Ophelia hadn't uttered a single word to the gentlemen. Highly irregular for her. Ophelia Breckensole was never at a loss for witticism or clever remarks, nor was she bashful.

Touching the brims of their hats, the dukes dipped their heads and murmured appropriate parting comments. However, as the Duke of Kincade reined his sleek mount around, he gave Rayne a covert wink.

Oh, he *was* a sly devil.

Had he arranged this whole charade?

If so, however had he talked Asherford into acting on his behalf?

Lord, what must Asherford think if it were true?

"We'd best hurry if we are to arrive at Nicolette's on time," Theadosia announced with her usual efficiency.

Happily discussing Nicolette's betrothal, the women advanced toward the entrance.

Once again entwining her hand in the crook of Rayne's elbow, Ophelia slowed her pace, holding them back a few steps.

Rayne sent her friend a questioning glance. They would be late, and given their close friendship with Nicolette and her exciting news, it would be the height of rudeness.

"I vow, Rayne Wellbrook, the Duke of Kincade winked at you." Eyes slightly narrowed, Ophelia stared at Rayne, a distinct discerning sparkle in her hazel gaze. "Do you dare deny it?"

Momentarily speechless, Rayne frantically muddled around in her mind for a feasible explanation. She seized upon the first thing certain to distract Ophelia. "Why were *you* ignoring Asherford?"

7

17 Bedford Square
That evening

Cutting into the perfectly cooked pancetta partridge in wine sauce, Fletcher veered a furtive glance toward Rayne, who was seated across and down two chairs from him. The seating arrangement made it impossible to speak with her and still observe dining propriety.

More inconvenient society rules.

Never speak across the table.

They did so at Levensyde House—at every meal, in point of fact. But then again, the Scots had never been as stodgy and formal as the English.

Which, he reluctantly admitted, was a good thing since he shouldn't indulge his wayward fascination with the vixen. Nothing could come of such a fixation. He wasn't such an unconscionable cad as to lead Rayne to believe there could be something between them, only to crush her hopes, as he surely must.

After all, he knew first hand that fragile English ladies and Scotland's demanding climate and pragmatic people did not blend well.

Oil and water.

Sawdust and ink.

Milk and tea.

What?

Nae, no' damned milk and tea.

Yer aff yer bloody heid.

Rayne could not be his. He'd never subject her or himself to such misery.

Toward that end, Fletcher had avoided her and even forbid himself to venture into his newly tidied gardens for fear he'd find himself peering over the wall like a moon-eyed swain.

The area near the folly remained more naturalized,

but he refused to admit he'd ordered it kept so for her. For if he admitted that—even if only to himself—then he'd have to acknowledge he felt something more than casual appreciation for the beautiful young woman.

Why then had he counted it his great good fortune that when he was on his way to Rotten Row with Asherford and San Sebastian earlier today, they'd come upon the women? More on point, why had Fletcher been inordinately pleased when Asherford had assumed he'd already been introduced to Rayne?

Because he knew full well that Asherford's presumption saved him from having to ask for the introduction as he'd stupidly told her he would do. Which was to say, he'd allowed himself an indulgence he could not afford. Which was to say, he could not pursue his burgeoning interest, even if Rayne Wellbrook was the most provocative, enticing, captivating, enthralling woman he'd met in…well, ever.

It is her damn enticing perfume.

Gardenia and carnation.

That was what had compelled him to vow he'd

arrange an introduction. The scent had muddled his reasoning.

And that is a colossal load of horse shite.

With her sable, bronze-and-gold-tinted hair caught up in an intricate design, a few glossy curls left to tease her ears, and wearing a mazarine blue satin gown accented with ivory lace and black velvet, Rayne was quite simply exquisite.

A single sapphire dangled from a black velvet ribbon tied at her neck. The hollow of her creamy throat tenderly nestled the sparkling gem. He was jealous as hell of the jewel.

Sapphire and pearl earrings hung from her dainty earlobes and swayed as she spoke or nodded. Each movement of the earbobs drew his attention to that delectable, perfumed juncture just below her ear that he'd almost tasted that day in his gardens.

Four times so far during the meal—but who was counting?—Fletcher caught Rayne studying him from beneath the dark fan of her eyelashes. However, upon each occurrence, she swiftly dropped her gaze to her plate. Not before adorable color had tinted her cheeks, causing the few equally adorable freckles to stand out.

His masculine pride swelled with primal satisfaction each time. He mercilessly deflated it with sordid memories of his mother's cold, cruel behavior and her venomous words.

If ever there were a perfect means to shrivel a partial cockstand—other than a good dousing in icy loch water—thoughts of his mother swiftly, succinctly, and thoroughly accomplished the task.

Regardless, Fletcher had slid so many brief, what he mistakenly believed were secretive, glances in Rayne's direction that Asherford had raised his noble brow and quirked his mouth up on one side into a mocking grin no less than five—*nae, there he goes again*—make that six times.

Slashing his brows together into a sod-off-and-go-bugger-yourself glare, Fletcher stabbed at a butter and herb covered carrot. And missed. One fat baby carrot rolled away while another skidded onto the edge of the plate, balanced for a blink, and then silently plopped onto the tablecloth.

His fork made a loud, grating noise as it scraped

across the gold-rimmed, pale moss-green china. The sound echoed loudly, and several guests turned curious gazes in his direction.

Heat billowed from Fletcher's waist to his hairline. With a low growl, he finally speared another runaway vegetable and stuffed it into his mouth whole. Honestly, he didn't even like carrots all that much, and he most especially didn't like the vegetable when it made him a fool.

Silent and stealthily as a ghost, a footman collected the runaway carrot. Nevertheless, an oily, herb-speckled stain marred the tablecloth.

Dammit.

Sheffield's shoulders shook with ill-concealed mirth, and his duchess, always the consummate hostess, opened and closed her mouth twice. As if she thought she should inquire after Fletcher but eschewed doing so as not to draw unwanted attention to him.

In the end, she offered an encouraging upward sweep of her mouth and speared her own carrot with superb ease. Without so much as the tiniest sound or sending a single tiny orange missile across the table, she cut a dainty bite-sized piece.

Egads, he felt as if he'd just been given a silent lesson in dining etiquette.

Hot humiliation stung Fletcher's cheeks, and another guttural noise echoed in his throat as he chewed. *Bloody damn.* He sounded like a primitive barbarian.

Hell, he *felt* like a primitive barbarian.

A barbarian who wanted to say to hell with reason and sensibleness, shove back his chair, sweep Rayne into his arms, and bundle her off to someplace secluded and private to explore whatever this burgeoning thing was between them.

Was it between them, or did he imagine her interest?

That galling thought settled like a glob of rancid bacon fat in his belly, and his fork hung limply in his hand as he reviewed their few interactions in his mind.

No, there *had* been a spark of interest in the magnificent depths of her coppery eyes. He hadn't imagined it.

"Your Grace?" Her pale blue eyes brimming with

kindness and concern, Jemmah, the lovely, strawberry-blonde Duchess of Dandridge, seated on his left asked, "Is something amiss?"

She pointed her gaze at his fork, hovering an inch above his plate.

"Nae. I simply slipped earlier."

What inane drivel.

A man who wielded a sword and a dirk with the skill Fletcher possessed did not *slip* with his fork. Until now, that was. Never had a woman distracted him as Rayne did.

Asherford coughed behind his serviette, and Sutcliffe and Sheffield, their mouths twitching, exchanged hilarity-filled glances before attending to the delicious meal once more.

Bloody idiots.

Fletcher attempted to remind himself precisely why they were friends, but at the moment, he couldn't summon a solitary reason why he'd been so buffleheaded as to befriend British dukes.

Puzzled frowns marred the usually smooth foreheads of several of the ladies as if they sensed the peculiar undercurrent but couldn't quite put their manicured fingers on what went on. However, they were astute women. If Fletcher wasn't more vigilant, he'd give himself away entirely.

Given the merriment and perceptive looks the married men at the table shared, he might've done so already.

Bloody, bloody hell.

At this rate, the entire assemblage would be onto Fletcher's inconvenient infatuation. And that presented a prickly situation he didn't want to explain. Nor did he wish Sheffield to approach him with questions he had no answers to. Well, not satisfactory answers that wouldn't have Sheffield calling him out for a cad and a bounder.

Therefore, for the remainder of the meal, Fletcher resolutely determined to keep his regard focused on his food, the Duchess of Dandridge on his left, and Ophelia Breckensole to his right.

He would not look across the table again.

Not even once.

What about after dinner when the gentleman had

finished with their cigars and brandy? When everyone came together in the drawing room, and there was not a table as a buffer between him and Rayne?

Fletcher would cross that milestone when he came to it.

Mayhap, he'd claim an early meeting or a forgotten issue that demanded his attention and depart directly after dining.

Poltroon. Coward.

No, he would not.

Fletcher would simply have to treat Rayne as he would any other debutante on the marriage mart.

Avoid her.

Remain coolly polite, detached, and unaffected.

He very much feared it was already far, *far* too late for any of that logic.

"Was I mistaken, Your Grace, or did you not wink at Rayne in Hyde Park earlier today?"

Miss Breckensole's barely audible inquiry meant for his ears alone sucked the air from his lungs.

Fletcher choked on the mouthful of wine he'd sipped to wash the taste of carrot from his palate and nearly spewed the contents onto the snowy white tablecloth. Stinging tears burned his eyes as he forced the fermented liquid down his constricted, convulsing throat.

Shite.

He'd never be asked to dine in Polite Society again.

Another thought—this one filled with abject dismay—came swiftly on the heels of the first.

She saw me.

Jesus.

Ye werena so verra suave after all, were ye?

Miss Ophelia Breckensole gazed at him, her face a mask of benign innocence. Yet behind her politesse, there was a glint of something else in the shrewd hazel eyes that she leveled at him. Something steely and relentless and unforgiving, despite the placid, demure countenance she presented.

How to answer her?

Christ, save me.

Salvation came from a wholly unforeseen source.

Asherford, seated on Miss Breckensole's other

side, unexpectantly queried, "Miss Breckensole, will you be attending the Gravenstones' masked ball next week? I'm going as a...a..."

Visibly struggling to summon a believable costume from thin air, his sharp gaze roved the room and settled jubilantly on the silk peacock-themed wallpaper.

"I'm going as a peacock," he blurted.

A...?

What the hell?

A peacock?

Peacock?

The hoot of laughter that jolted to Fletcher's throat damned near strangled him. He swiftly covered his mouth, but a muffled sound very much like a dying squirrel emerged nonetheless.

Flying vegetables. Screeching forks. Choking on wine. Making peculiar sounds?

Aye, just what every hostess desired at a dinner party.

For certain, he'd never be invited to dine by anyone in the *ton* again.

He didn't give a hog's grunt.

"Peacocks are quite intelligent," Asherford improvised.

Like hell, they were. Every peafowl Fletcher had ever encountered had been noisy, aggressive, and dull-witted as a turnip.

Miss Breckensole speared Asherford with what could only be called an impatient—perhaps even annoyed if she weren't so well-mannered—half-glance.

Asherford had effortlessly drawn Miss Breckensole's attention from Fletcher, and, in doing so, had handily entrapped himself. God Almighty, the incongruity was nothing short of hilarious. He now understood the mirth enjoyed by his friends at his expense earlier.

For the truth of it was that Asherford did not *blurt* anything. The man was as sparing with his carefully articulated words as a miser was with a shilling. He also loathed—absolutely abhorred—masquerade balls. He'd voiced his contempt for the ridiculous assemblages numerous times.

And to save Fletcher further awkwardness—likely Rayne as well, if Asherford had also seen Fletcher's wink earlier today—he'd committed to attending the Gravenstones' ball. The most garish and absurdly decorated gathering hosted every Season. What was more, Asherford had declared he'd go as a flamboyant fowl.

By God, Fletcher might also have to put in an appearance just to see Asherford's tall, somber form strutting about as a peafowl.

Priceless. That was going to be bloody priceless.

Another snicker threatened, but Fletcher squelched it. Instead, schooling his expression into what he hoped was one of appreciation, he sent his friend a grateful smile and mouthed a silent thank you over the top of Miss Breckensole's head.

"So is Kincade," Asherford continued with a wickedly skewed eyebrow and sly sideways grin. "Attending as a peacock, that is."

Not so bloody damned noble or sacrificial after all. If Asherford must endure the most godawful ball of the Season, then so would Fletcher. One for all and all for one. Down with the ship and all that courageous rot.

In truth, Fletcher had nearly gone down with a ship a decade ago.

Before his father had died, he'd enjoyed a short, dangerous stint as a privateer. That was the year he'd rebelled at being born a ducal heir. More than anything else, he'd taken to the seas as a scandalous buccaneer as revenge toward his mother.

He'd known she'd despise his doing so, and he continued to wear the earring for the same reason. It absolutely infuriated her, which she made known regularly.

"Really, Kincade," she reproved in that shrill, hoity-toity tone that scraped along his nerves and made him want to shove his fingers in his ears like a petulant child. "*Must* you wear that evidence"—long, elegant fingers flicked with perfectly shaped oval nails toward the earring—"of your unfortunate decision?"

Aye, indeed, dear Mother, I must.

The truth of the matter was that the privateer he sailed upon had nearly been scuttled by a pirate ship.

An old, much more experienced sea salt, Wen Ling, had saved Fletcher from pitching over the side and to certain death.

Fletcher put a finger to the band, recalling the sailor's urgent and sincere warning.

Wen Ling had pointed to the earring in his left ear, and in his lyrical accented voice, explained that his life had been endangered too. According to an ancient Chinese legend, one who wore an earring in their left ear had already faced death and escaped. The earring was worn as a talisman to protect against a recurrence. Then, he'd not only gifted Fletcher the earring he now wore, but Wen Ling had also pierced his ear.

With a whalebone needle.

It had hurt like hell.

The old memory kicked Fletcher's mouth upward on one side the merest bit.

That wasn't the only reason he wore the earring, however. The band also reminded him why he couldn't be the same kind of fool the prior duke had been.

"In fact, all of the dukes are," Asherford announced smugly.

Bringing his mind back to the present, Fletcher focused on Asherford.

Still going on about that masked ball twaddle, was he?

"Are what?" Forehead wrinkled in confusion, Jules, the Duke of Dandridge, broke protocol about only speaking with those on his immediate right or left.

"Yes, what precisely are we doing?" Sheffield inquired, reaching for his wine and sending San Sebastian and Waycross inquisitive looks.

Knife and fork midair, San Sebastian shrugged. "The devil if I ken."

"I dinna ken either." A vexed expression was stamped upon Waycross's craggy features. But the brusque Scot was annoyed most of the time, so that was nothing new.

It seemed all of the dukes had decided to eschew etiquette.

The image of the dukes swaggering into Gravenstones' ball, each with a swath of brightly colored feather attached to their heads and backsides, nearly sent Fletcher into another fit of guffaws.

Before Miss Breckensole turned and responded to Asherford, she flicked a meaningful glance between Fletcher and Rayne.

His jollity promptly evaporated.

This was no empty-headed miss with stars in her eyes. No, indeed. Miss Breckensole was too astute by far. Leveling him a cool stare, she murmured a stern warning beneath her breath. "Do *not* do *anything* to hurt her. You do not know what she has been through."

Fletcher blinked rather owlishly.

What the devil did she mean by that?

What had Rayne gone through?

He slid her a sideways glance before giving the slightest nod.

Giving him a tightlipped smile, Miss Breckensole quite unenthusiastically attended Asherford, whose eyes lit up with masculine possessiveness.

Och, what goes on here?

Fletcher's curiosity was short-lived because the Duchess of Dandridge said as she adeptly cut a bite of partridge, "I had the pleasure of having tea with your mother at Lady St. Lavelle's yesterday. I understand felicitations are in order, Your Grace."

He puzzled his brow. "Felicitations?"

For what?

Letting the house at 19 Belford Square?

Was that truly something worth congratulating?

Mayhap Her Grace mistakenly believed he'd purchased the place. Which, in truth, he had decided was a good investment and had already asked Leith MacKettrick, his man of affairs, to send an inquiry to the owners to see if they were interested in selling the property.

"I beg your pardon." Her face fell, and she sent an anxious glance around the table as if she'd committed a *faux pas*. "I was unaware your betrothal hadn't been announced."

8

17 Bedford Square

Two days later in the late afternoon

R ayne ran her fingers through the cool water as she slowly wandered around the fountain. Where she wished to be—anywhere but here—and where she actually was—London—were two vastly different things. She might've gone shopping with Everleigh and Sarah, Griffin's ward, and to Gunter's afterward, but neither outing had appealed overly much.

Nothing had appealed to her since overhearing the Duchess of Dandridge congratulate Fletcher on his betrothal. Rayne didn't need one guess, much less three, to know who the fortunate lady was.

A vision of sun-kissed hair, a flawless peach complexion, and narrowed, unkind blue eyes intruded. Snobbish, conceited, vile tempered, black-hearted Lady Cecelia Sheldon-Furnsby.

In Lady Sheldon-Furnsby's case, beauty was truly only skin deep. From Rayne's few interactions, she'd deduced her ladyship was foul to her black-hearted core. All the pretty outward wrapping couldn't disguise her ugly soul.

Not only was Rayne dismayed that Fletcher hadn't been forthcoming with her about his relationship with Lady Sheldon-Furnsby, but she was also disappointed in his choice of a wife. She hadn't believed him so shallow as to choose a vain, shallow, self-centered termagant like Lady Sheldon-Furnsby.

But, then again, Rayne shouldn't have been surprised. Lady Sheldon-Furnsby possessed everything that High Society valued in a duchess: beauty, breeding, and wealth. Throw in her position and powerful connections and one had a veritable treasure trove of attributes. None of which made her a decent person.

Regardless, Fletcher had chosen her to become his duchess.

Rayne couldn't envision the persnickety beauty leaving London's luxuries and entertainment behind for Scotland. Not that there was anything wrong with Scotland. It wasn't as if the land north of England was occupied by uncivilized barbarians. Though she'd only ever seen paintings, Rayne thought the raw beauty of the country immensely appealing.

Neither could she see Fletcher remaining in London indefinitely. Unlike the fops and dandies that often paraded around the city, he was too rugged and untamed. Too powerfully built and muscled to ever pass for an English peer. Not, she was quite certain, that he had any wish to.

Besides, she rather suspected he not only preferred but needed the less rigorous strictures Scotland provided a man like him. Either Lady Sheldon-Furnsby or Fletcher was going to be utterly miserable.

Rayne shook her head.

No, eventually, both would be unhappy. It

couldn't be helped. If one married someone who wasn't content unless their spouse acquiesced to their every want and whim, stifling their own desires and needs, then bitterness and resentment would inevitably arise. Those dark sentiments would eventually smother any surviving joy and happiness.

Perhaps neither Fletcher nor his betrothed cared about any of that. There were those who entered into arranged unions who didn't give a fig.

Rayne very much cared about such things.

It was also possible, she supposed, theirs was a marriage of convenience, and they'd keep separate residences. That wasn't uncommon among aristocrats. This only further proved Rayne didn't know Fletcher McQuinton, Duke of Kincade at all.

But then, how could she have in under a week's acquaintance?

For certain, she'd naively read too much into their unexpected encounter in his gardens and at Hyde Park too.

More fool she.

At least she'd learned of his perfidy early on.

Before her heart had become fully engaged. There was that blessing to be grateful for.

Rayne blamed her ignorance on her inexperience. Until meeting Fletcher, she'd been content without romantic male attention. In point of fact, prior to him, any man who'd taken a more than casual interest in her had straight-up terrified her.

Sighing, she removed a gray feather with black markings from the fountain's uppermost level. In that insignificant gesture, she'd save Fitzroy a degree of frustration. This feather belonged to an Eurasian dove.

Glancing upward, she frowned at the stern disapproval permanently etched upon Apollo's marble features. Giving in to a childish whim and her discontented mood, she stuck her tongue out at the statue.

Why had the artist cast the god in such a dark temperament?

Who wanted to be forever memorialized as a grump?

Circling the fountain again, Rayne passed the bench where she'd abandoned her sketching. Even that pleasurable pastime hadn't been able to hold her attention because, despite her determination otherwise, her mind wandered to that day she'd intended to draw the wisteria.

And that, of course, led to more ruminations about Fletcher.

She'd lost track of how many times she'd gone around and around the small courtyard.

Her dratted musings kept drifting to him.

Fletcher McQuinton, Duke of Kincade.

Scoundrel? Rapscallion? Rake? Womanizer?

The sort of man who flirted with one woman even as he intended to ask another to wed him?

She wouldn't have believed it of him, but the truth was self-evident. An unladylike snort escaped her. She didn't care. *Damn him.* Even knowing his true character and admitting she'd escaped entanglement with a cad, Rayne couldn't deny he'd enchanted her.

Still did, truth be told.

And that makes you a nincompoop, Rayne Wellbrook.

It did, indeed.

From that very first devastating smile in Fletcher's garden, he'd caught her in his silky, seductive web. Obviously, the enchantment was one-sided.

He hadn't even bid her farewell two nights ago.

Citing an important matter that needed his immediate attention, Fletcher had taken his leave directly after dessert. For the life of her, Rayne couldn't conceive what had arisen during the meal that required his attention.

Perchance he'd only just remembered something urgent.

Yes, that he was betrothed.

Pressing her lips into a hard line, she kicked at an errant pebble. It tumbled across the pavers, coming to rest beneath one of the benches.

Perhaps Fletcher was a coward after all and had wanted nothing more than to escape her accusatory glances.

Had she sent him accusatory glances?

If so, they'd been unintentional. Pray to God no one else had noticed.

In point of fact, Rayne had endeavored not to look

at him anymore after the Duchess of Dandridge's inadvertent announcement. But as conversations are wont to do, a perfectly timed lull enabled everyone sitting near Fletcher, and she suspected along the entire lengths of both sides of the table, to hear her grace's apology.

Rayne's wounded heart gave a queer flip that she felt clear to her belly.

Remorse? Hurt?

Regret for what might've been?

She honestly didn't know.

Filling her lungs, she held her breath and closed her eyes. Then, slowly counting to ten, she released the air. She'd learned that calming behavior years ago and rarely had to call upon it anymore.

Why, then, couldn't she shake this melancholy?

For pity's sake, Fletcher owed her nothing. *Nothing*.

They both knew it.

Rayne had conceded that fact readily. If she hadn't been sneaking onto the property next door, they would never have had that clandestine meeting. A romantic at heart, she'd foolishly hoped the encounter and his rakish wink in Hyde Park had meant more.

It hadn't.

Not to a practiced rogue such as he, it hadn't, in any event.

A graceful clouded yellow butterfly flitted by a few feet over Rayne's head, catching her attention.

Remembering the vow she'd made the day she'd encountered Fletcher to sketch the next clouded yellow she saw, she snatched up her abandoned art supplies and trotted after the winged beauty as it gracefully flitted to and fro. Instead of stopping to drink from the scabious as she'd anticipated it would, the butterfly continued onward toward the rose-covered arbor.

"Where are you going?" Rayne muttered aloud, hurrying after the insect.

She gasped in delight when she turned the bend in the pathway and beheld at least a dozen clouded yellows hovering around the arbor and nearby scarlet beebalm.

"Ah, did you know I've been in the doldrums, and you brought me here to cheer me?" she asked the butterfly.

The notion was preposterous, and with so many butterflies gliding about, she had no idea which one she'd followed. However, the spectacle before her was breathtaking—like something from a fairyland. Never before had she seen so many clouded yellow butterflies in one place.

"I hoped ye'd come," a familiar burr resonated from within the arbor as a tall form emerged.

Oh, God.

At least this time, Rayne didn't shriek like a banshee.

As he had that first day, Fletcher wore buckskins tucked into Hessians. Today, however, he wore a coat—a deep burgundy accented with gold braid and trim. If she'd thought he'd looked like a swashbuckler with his shirtsleeves rolled to his elbows the other day, she'd been sorely mistaken.

This version of a roguish buccaneer was wholly mesmerizing.

A bicorn hat rested upon his head, his loose hair brushing his ridiculously broad shoulders. A dirk protruded from the top of his left boot, giving him a rakish, devil-may-care appearance.

He quite took her breath away. For several rapid heartbeats, all she could do was stare, taking in each magnificent contour and plane of him. As it always did, his masculine beauty stirred something primal and powerful deep within her. For the first time, Rayne felt herself wishing a man—*this man*—might be hers for all time.

She'd finally found a man she wasn't afraid of, a man she was attracted to, a man she had undefinable feelings for, and he belonged to another.

Wouldn't you know it?

Whoever had said fate or destiny was a cruel mistress hadn't been exaggerating.

Marshaling her thoughts and composure, she said, "Fletcher? I mean, Your Grace?"

It came out a question.

"Rayne."

He addressed her by her given name, and her gullible heart took to wing over such a trivial, insignificant thing.

Holding her sketch pad to her chest and clutching her pencils, she eased forward. A smile tipped the corner of her mouth. Last time she'd used a basket as a shield.

"Whatever are you doing in the arbor?" She cut the enclosure a swift glance before focusing on him again.

"Waitin' for ye."

"Waiting…for me?"

At that moment, she fell a little bit in love with him.

And yet she knew full well that doing so was foolhardy. Not only did he belong to another, but he also couldn't have known she'd venture out here today.

Peering up at him, noting the shadow of a beard forming on his chiseled jaw, Rayne said as much. "That was awfully silly of you. I don't normally spend time in these gardens in the afternoon. It gets too warm, and Everleigh worries that I'll freckle. You might've waited for hours, and I wouldn't have come."

Her aunt was blessed with extremely fair hair and creamy skin that she diligently protected from the sun.

Whereas Rayne must've had a freckled ancestor with red hair perched in her family tree somewhere.

"I dinna mind the wait." Fletcher lifted a broad shoulder, his keen blue-green gaze roaming over her. Almost…almost as if he hungered for the sight of her too. "I kent Sheffield was out this afternoon, and it was safe to venture here."

Only if Fitzroy or one of the other gardeners didn't come upon him and raise a hue and cry.

No doubt, Griffin had made an offhand remark about his plans for the afternoon during another of his meetings with Fletcher today. She could hardly ask him not to mention such things to the Duke of Kincade without raising questions as to why she didn't want their neighbor and Griffin's business associate to know.

Not only would Rayne sound like an illogical idiot, she would put Fletcher in danger of Griffin's wrath if he learned what had transpired between her and Fletcher, no matter how innocent.

For certain, she'd never divulged a word intentionally. She didn't think he would either.

"I hoped ye'd feel the urge to wander the gardens." Fletcher clasped his hands behind his back in the manner of someone who was nervous and wanted to conceal their uneasiness.

What an absurd notion.

Men of his ilk were never nervous around women.

"I ken ye dinna feel ye can visit my gardens anymore, though I've told ye, ye are welcome to any time." A half-smile bent his mouth and creased the corners of his eyes. "I've made an offer to purchase the house and am awaitin' word from the owner."

"Oh."

How could her heart simultaneously soar and plummet?

Any hope that she'd be able to resume her visits to her former oasis was permanently crushed. And yet, the knowledge that Fletcher would be in residence on occasion thrilled her much more than it ought to. Assuredly more than was reasonable or wise. Especially as Lady Sheldon-Furnsby would be their new neighbor as well, only she'd be the Duchess of Kincade then.

Rayne doubted very much she'd venture near the garden wall ever again. Not with that virago living next door. The new duchess would probably insist the grounds become enthusiastically weeded and pruned formal gardens.

The notion made Rayne queasy. At least she told herself it was the ruination of her oasis that sickened her rather than who Fletcher would share her former sanctuary with.

The best course might be to press Everleigh and Griffin into permitting her to return to Fittledale Park. Yes, that was the very thing. Rayne was of age, and she could insist she leave London.

"I intend to have my brother and sister to stay with me if they are amenable," Fletcher said, all polished politesse and formality.

"I see," she managed, despising this stiltedness that had sprung up between them. It hadn't been like that their first meeting, nor when he'd come upon her in Hyde Park. She forced herself to focus on the present. "I trust you were able to settle your urgent matter."

"Aye. It's been dealt with."

He didn't offer details, and she wasn't intrusive or bold enough to ask. Likely it was a matter related to his business dealings—transactions that most men erroneously believed a woman incapable of understanding.

Fletcher drew nearer, his striking eyes intense and probing.

"Lass?" He stopped and firmed his mouth, his expression inscrutable. "I ken ye heard what the Duchess of Dandridge said the other night."

Rayne stiffened her spine and lifted her chin, more to brace herself against any possible hurt his next words might inflict than any affront at the unpleasant subject.

"I did," she admitted without preamble.

She would not reference the sensual interlude they'd shared several days ago. In all fairness, perhaps he hadn't been betrothed yet.

Well, he was close to becoming affianced and had no business flirting with you. Whispering in your ear. Vowing he wanted an introduction. Causing you to hope…

Hope *what* exactly?

Rayne hadn't even defined what the *what* was. It was an unnamed, unidentified *something*. Which was to say, a big nothing now. Suddenly feeling incredibly hot and tired, and wishing this discomfiting encounter to end, she brushed her hair off her face. "What is it you want, Your Grace?"

As she had that day nearly a week ago, she wore her hair down. The afternoon had grown quite warm, and she moved past him toward the arbor, welcoming its cooling shade. Welcoming the added distance between them just as much.

For when Fletcher was near, it was as if he were a magnet. Her body swayed toward him, her feet itched to close the space separating them, and she yearned to wrap her arms about his slim torso and lay her cheek on the wide expanse of his chest.

All of which were preposterous and impossible.

God, how could these feelings even exist?

She'd only known this man for a week. One very short week. Seven days.

"It is inappropriate for us to be alone," she reminded him again, striving to put emotional distance between them too. "And more so as you are newly betrothed."

Following her, he stepped into the shadows behind her. The scent of roses hung heavy and cloying in the slightly cooler air.

"Lass, I'm no' betrothed. I never have been."

Her ridiculous heart leaped at his quiet pronouncement.

Stupid, imprudent, rash hope sprang anew.

These emotional ups and downs were wreaking havoc on her.

"I don't understand," Rayne said, shaking her head and narrowing her eyes. What game did he play? "I quite clearly heard her grace offer you felicitations and apologize for revealing your betrothal before an official announcement had been made."

So had everyone else at the table, if the immediate buzz that had broken out was any indication.

It was Fletcher's turn to shake his head, his steady, unrepentant gaze holding hers captive. She was snared, unable to look away, like a mouse in a trap. "Nae, she'd been misinformed."

Misinformed?

A betrothal wasn't something trite or inconsequential that someone might be mistaken about. For instance, whether Lady Jersey took milk with her tea, or the sun had shone sixteen days last month, or Prinny's favorite color was pink.

Rayne had heard that last triviality somewhere, not that the Prince Regent's favorite color mattered to her in the least.

Fletcher's engagement *did* matter, however.

Either one was betrothed, or one was not.

Which was it?

Framed in the arbor's opening, with the profusion of roses surrounding him and butterflies flitting about behind him, he looked like a prince from one of Nicolette's naughty romantic novels.

From the first moment—all right, mayhap not the *first* moment—Rayne had believed Fletcher unlike other men. Had perhaps unfairly plopped him on a pedestal—*a very short pedestal it turned out*—and attributed characteristics to him and expectations of him that were impractical.

Gesturing to the bench, he said, "Why dinna ye sit down, and I'll explain."

Because Rayne so wanted to believe him—and she'd realized when it came to Fletcher McQuinton, Duke of Kincade, she was malleable as fresh bread dough—she obediently sank onto the unyielding stone bench. After setting aside her sketching supplies and arranging her simple sea-foam green skirts, she primly folded her hands in her lap and crossed her ankles.

With a start, she realized she was holding her breath. Gradually releasing the pent-up air, she canted her head. "What is it you wish to say, Your Grace? Be quick about it, please. As I've told you before, I cannot risk ruination."

In truth, ruination might get her sent packing back to Fittledale Park. Honestly, that didn't seem such a horrid punishment.

Yes, but any chance you'd ever have at a respectable match and having children would be forever destroyed.

Why wasn't that true for unmarried men too?

Unfair, her heart cried.

Men were praised and touted as conquerors for their sexual triumphs, while unmarried women were disgraced for all time for simply being found alone with a man. They became pariahs, someone to be shuffled off to a country estate or a discreet cottage.

Debutantes were expected to remain untouched and virginal while young bucks could rut like stags or bulls without consequence.

Pausing in her rueful ruminations, Rayne scrunched her nose.

Did she want a match?

Truthfully, she wasn't certain.

Her past still held her partially imprisoned and made contemplating a future difficult. Nevertheless, she adored babies—their sweet smell and so, so soft skin—and was positive that she wanted children. Furthermore, she was fully prepared to perform her wifely duties with her husband to acquire said children, no matter how distasteful the intimacy may be.

Rayne slid Fletcher a sideways glance.

Intimacy with him wouldn't be a chore at all. She was positive about that as well. A flush of mortification engulfed her, and she waved her hand before her face.

"Goodness, it's awfully warm. How can you bear the heat with that coat?"

He lifted one shoulder an crooked a smile. "I spent time in the tropics. This heat doesn't begin to compare to those stifling temperatures and humidity."

That diverted her attention. "Did you truly?"

"Aye. As a privateer." He flicked a long finger at his earring, barely visible through his thick hair hanging to his shoulders. "That's when I acquired this."

"How fascinating." It truly was. How did a duke become a privateer? Or was it the other way around? "I'd love to hear about your travels and how you came to have your earring."

Stop. Don't encourage him. You shouldn't even be having this little tête-à-tête.

Ah, yes.

Scandal and disgrace awaited her if they were

caught. Not to mention, Griffin would likely feel obliged to call Fletcher out. Why did men always think violence was the answer to disagreements? If women ran the world, Rayne was convinced there'd be far fewer wars.

She peered anxiously out the arbor's opening. It wasn't probable that anyone would come upon them, but it wasn't impossible either.

Fletcher settled his large form beside hers, his granite-hard thigh brushing her gown just inches from her leg. This near, his clean, manly scent wafted to her.

Slightly spicy. Cloves?

She filled her lungs.

And a woodsy aroma.

Pine? Eucalyptus? Juniper?

Tucking her hair behind her ears, she faced him. And waited.

He'd sought her out after all.

Chin tucked to his chest, Fletcher appeared deep in reflection. He scratched beneath his lower lip with his thumbnail. At long last, he sighed and removed his hat. Laying it atop his knee, he rested his head against the arbor and gazed upward.

Weariness radiated from him, and Rayne wanted to brush back the errant lock of hair that had tumbled over his forehead when he'd scooped his hat off.

Hands clasped tightly to prevent any such unwise action, she continued to wait.

Without looking at her, he said, "The Duchess of Dandridge was purposely misinformed. Lady St. Lavelle spoke out of turn when she declared her daughter and I were to wed. I havena offered for Lady Sheldon-Furnsby's hand, nor do I intend to. Ever."

Resolution and conviction thickened his brogue and deepened the timbre of his voice.

Angling his head, he caught Rayne's eye, and a tender smile bent his mouth.

She forbade her heart to skip about excitedly.

This was a serious business.

Furrowing her forehead, she put a finger to her cheek. The tale was so farfetched and fanciful that she was hard-pressed to believe him. But what motivation had he to lie to her about such a thing? Denying a betrothal was scandalous behavior. His good name would have a black mark upon it. Well, mayhap a slight smudge. Not that most of Society would care. Dukes could do no wrong.

"Are you suggesting she made the whole tale up?" Rayne spread her hands wide, bumping his shoulder. "Beg your pardon," she mumbled, returning her hands to her lap.

A short grunt was Fletcher's only response.

She wasn't finished, however, and needed to be perfectly clear on the matter.

"Am I to believe her ladyship fabricated that nonsensical tripe and spread it about as if it were true? That was dreadfully bold and risky. Did she hope to entrap you?"

"Aye. Lady St. Lavelle and my mother are old friends. The two put their conniving' heads together and hatched the scheme."

Rayne plopped back against the bench. Why, she couldn't imagine such interfering parents. Her mother had died too young to meddle in Rayne's life, and Everleigh was all that was protective and considerate.

"That's…that's simply dreadful, Fletcher. I am

truly sorry." The latter seemed wholly inadequate. "Will they decry you and claim you broke the betrothal?"

Giving a derisive chuckle, Fletcher scrubbed a big hand over his jaw. His knuckles sported several ebony hairs.

"'Tis dangerous thwartin' two strong-minded women, and I unwisely underestimated their deviousness. It willna happen again. They've desired a match between Cecelia—Lady Sheldon-Furnsby—and me for years. I've steadfastly refused."

He wasn't lying. She could see it in the resolve stamped upon his features.

"If Christ himself appeared and ordered me to wed Cecelia, I'd respectfully decline our Lord's directive," he said. "I shall never, under any circumstances, wed her."

Steel underlaid Fletcher's tone and the vehemence with which he made the harsh declaration.

"Why?" Rayne could've bitten off her tongue, yet genuine curiosity compelled her to ask. There wasn't anything about this man she didn't want to know.

Fletcher pointed his gaze overhead again and said nothing for an extended moment. So long, in fact, Rayne concluded he wouldn't answer her prying question. The buzz of industrious bees accented the silence, and just when she was about to excuse herself to go inside, he finally replied.

"I dinna care for her in the way a man ought to for the woman he takes to wife."

So Fletcher McQuinton was a romantic after all?

Had his parents' marriage been a love match and he desired the same sort of union? Rayne's father had died when she was but two years old. Nevertheless, her mother had spoken of him often—always with a faraway, dreamy gleam in her eyes.

In the muted light, Rayne searched Fletcher's dear face. His stiffly held jaw, the tense lines framing his mouth, and the involuntary flexing of the inner corners of his eyebrows betrayed his continued disquiet.

There was something he wasn't saying.

"What else, Fletcher?"

He took her hand in his large palm and brushed his thumb back and forth across the top. The gesture wasn't the least sexual, but her body came to life, from her peaked nipples pushing against her chemise to her damp woman's center.

Rayne ought to have been mortified at her immediate sensual response, but she wasn't.

Only he had the power to do that to her.

Of its own accord, her attention drifted to his mouth. That dashed beautiful mouth.

She captured her lower lip between her teeth, praying he couldn't read her wicked thoughts.

"Rayne?"

She glanced upward, meeting his smoldering gaze. Liquid blue-green fire blazed there.

"Yes?" she breathed, knowing before he said the words—nay hoping, praying—exactly what he would say.

"I want to kiss ye."

"Oh, yes. Please."

Did one say please in a moment such as this?

Did doing so make Rayne seem too desperate? A wanton?

The smile arcing his mouth made her questions

and her qualms melt away like a lump of sugar in hot tea.

Tenderly cupping her cheek with one hand, Fletcher pulled her into his iron-like embrace with the other. She reveled in his steely arm surrounding her. Solid and firm and masculine perfection. So much more than she'd ever let herself imagine when she did daydream about a man holding her. Kissing her. Loving her with his body.

The last generally brought her plummeting unpleasantly back to reality.

Fletcher stared into her eyes for an interminable moment, the seconds dragging by in concert to the bees.

Buzz. Buzz. Buzz.

Then with a small smile playing around the edges of his lips, his eyelids drifted shut, and he covered her mouth with his.

Bliss. Pure bliss.

Rayne released a ragged sigh and, looping her arms about his corded neck, sagged into him and kissed him back.

His tongue lazily played with hers, tasting and exploring.

Unlike the disgusting kiss forced upon her when she was fifteen, he didn't plunge his tongue into her mouth and make her gag. Nor did he roughly grope her breasts or mash her bottom.

He tasted of mint and fruit and Fletcher—not onions and spirits and unbrushed teeth.

Wanting their kiss to go on forever, Rayne melted further into him—until she was unsure where she ended and he began. She lost track of time—lost track of what was right and wrong. Forgot to be afraid or worry about her reputation.

And that was saying something indeed.

Fletcher was her world—her universe. He was all that mattered at this moment.

Every minute they spent in each other's arms made her want more. Like a woman starved, she took everything he generously offered, and it still wasn't enough.

"Fletcher," she moaned against his mouth, arching into him.

At last, he broke away and, with his forehead pressed against hers, his breathing rasping and fitful, he said, "Nae more, *lèannan*. I canna control myself with ye. Ye are intoxicatin'. An irresistible aphrodisiac, Rayne Wellbrook."

Intoxicating? An aphrodisiac?

Her?

Me?

And just like that, in the blink of an eye, as bees and butterflies drank nectar from fat blossoms, two more pieces of her heart became his.

It wasn't until she lay in her bed late that night, reliving their kisses, that she recalled he'd never told her the *what else* she'd asked about.

What secret did he guard as fervently as she guarded hers?

9

19 Bedford Square
One week later

T he next week passed in a blur of activity as Fletcher's first ship was outfitted, her crew hired, and the *Misty Morning*—Florence's choice for the ship's name—was readied to sale to India. The ship would return with spices, silk, linen, and tea, and hopefully the next ship—as yet unnamed—would be nearly ready to outfit as well.

He'd also written Greg and Florence, inviting them to come to London. It was too soon for a response, but he informed them that he had no immediate plans to return to Scotland. He would, of course, do so eventually. He wanted to. Just not quite yet.

A wry grin slanted his mouth.

A fortnight ago, he couldn't wait to shake London's coal dust from his boots. Now, however, thanks to an endearing, winsome wood nymph, he wasn't sure when he'd leave. More on point, when he did eventually return home, would Rayne accompany him?

Conflict still raged within him about formally courting her. If he asked to pay his addresses, Sheffield would rightly expect a marriage proposal to be forthcoming.

Truthfully, Fletcher yearned to marry Rayne.

That knowledge horrified and delighted him.

And yet, a genuine terror that he'd make the same mistake his father had and that Rayne might end up as miserable and bitter as his mother kept him mute.

Rayne is nothin' like Mother. Nothin'.

That inarguable truth was what kept Fletcher seeking Miss Rayne Wellbrook's charming company. They'd shared three more clandestine garden meetings at the Sheffields'—each instigated by him. Citing her reputation and gossiping servants for her reluctance, Rayne steadfastly refused to come over the wall to his property again.

Though she eagerly responded to his kisses, he sensed she held something back. That she never completely let herself go. Fletcher wanted to ask her about her reservations, but doing so hardly seemed appropriate as they weren't affianced, and he'd vowed to himself to not go beyond passionate kisses.

His bloody honor and that damnable pledge might be the death of him.

Could a man die of a permanent erection?

Nonetheless, his passion and desire for Rayne had become a raging inferno. He'd summoned Herculean restraint to keep their interludes to kissing and nothing more. By God, he wouldn't tup her in a cramped garden arbor.

If she became his duchess, he'd go about introducing her to lovemaking properly in an oversized bed covered in yellow satin sheets—because, after all, yellow was her favorite color. He'd fill 19 Bedford

Square's gardens with yellow roses and every other imaginable yellow flower there was.

Sunflowers. Foxgloves. Primroses. Daffodils. Dahlias. Daisies. Marigolds. Hollyhocks...

The current owner of the house had insisted on meeting with Fletcher in person, which meant a trip to Warwick. Elliot Pritchard, a lean, handsome, soft-spoken man at perhaps the end of his sixth decade, desired to know why Fletcher wished to buy the house.

Quite irregular, truth be told.

Typically, sellers only cared about how much they could gain from the sale of their property. Though Pritchard's request struck Fletcher as unusual and the timing was inconvenient for a long day trip to Warwick, he'd acquiesced.

Mostly because he wanted the damned house.

Wanted it because of the minx who lived next door.

Every night, often with a tumbler of whisky in hand, he stood in his—well, Pritchard's— fragrant garden and gazed toward 17 Bedford Square. It had taken Fletcher three days, but he'd finally identified

Rayne's third-story bedchamber. Centered between the other chambers, hers looked out onto the gardens.

He'd suspected it might, and his diligence had paid off.

She often pulled the draperies aside and, in her nightclothes with that glorious hair, a burnished curtain around her slender shoulders, gazed out onto the garden. Or mayhap, it was the night sky that intrigued her. Or…perchance—and he desperately wished that were the case—she looked into his gardens, hoping to catch a glimpse of him.

Over a cup of delicious oolong tea, he'd shared the story of Rayne's visits to the gardens with Mr. Pritchard. How, in such a short time, she'd come to mean a great deal to him. That, Fletcher admitted aloud for the first time, he was seriously contemplating making her his duchess.

"Honestly, Mr. Pritchard, I canna bear the thought of anyone else livin' in the house now." Chuckling, Fletcher raked his fingers through his hair. "The place has bewitched me."

Och, the vixen in the house next door had, for

certain.

One knee flung across the other as he relaxed into the tufted cranberry-red velvet chair he sat in, Mr. Pritchard took a sip of his steaming tea, intently regarding Fletcher over the rim of the dainty cup the whole while. A nascent smile tipped his mouth upward as he effortlessly placed the cup into its matching saucer.

"You haven't asked about the stairs on either side of the wall, Your Grace."

Fletcher paused in bringing a Shrewsbury biscuit to his mouth.

"I had assumed they were installed when the houses were built." Fletcher quirked an eyebrow upward. "Do ye ken their origins?"

"I do indeed," Mr. Pritchard replied with another one of his sad, distracted smiles.

Och, out with it, man. Do I have to beg ye?

Fletcher cleared his throat and opened his mouth, prepared to do that very thing. He needed to be on his way soon if he meant to reach London by nightfall.

"Many years ago—oh, it must be close to three-

and-thirty now—two people fell in love," Mr. Pritchard said.

Fletcher settled back into his chair, prepared to listen to what was in all likelihood a long tale. If that was what it took for Pritchard to sell him the place, he'd stay all bloody damned night.

"Their families would've heartily disapproved had they been aware," Pritchard said, the merest bit of cynicism or conceivably it was bitterness leeching into his words. "Society would have as well. It didn't matter to them. They bought houses side by side on Bedford Square and installed the steps so they might secretly rendezvous."

Now that took some ballocks.

Usually, discretion was expected, even for affairs or the keeping of a mistress. Fletcher had never kept a paramour. Oh, he'd enjoyed bed sport on many occasions, but he didn't go around swiving everything in skirts.

"For nearly three decades," Pritchard continued softly as if he was seeing into the past, "they were as happy as anyone in their situation might be."

Fletcher couldn't help but wonder why the lovers didn't just use the kitchen doors. It was much easier than climbing the wall, particularly as the people had to be nearing fifty if they carried on an affair for thirty years.

Mr. Pritchard fell silent, tapping his long fingers upon his grey-striped clad knee as he stared out the window, sorrow etching shadows in his features. He'd fallen into several of those weighty silences during the visit.

"I presume one of them, or perhaps both, were already married?" Fletcher said in an attempt to get him speaking again. He had a long ride ahead of him, and that seemed the most logical reason for two people unable to marry and make a life for themselves.

Mr. Pritchard brought his grey-eyed gaze to meet Fletcher's squarely, a bold challenge in his eyes.

"No, Your Grace. Neither was ever married."

What?

Never...?

Fletcher regarded him, then comprehension dawned.

Och. That was the way of it then.

He made an affirming sound in his throat. Sensing that this wasn't the end of the tale, he waited uncomplainingly for Mr. Pritchard to go on.

"Five years ago, Terrance Blakely died from cancer. His death came swiftly, with little warning. Three-and-twenty days, in fact. It gave me far too little time to prepare for life without him."

That bloody quickly?

"I simply couldn't bear to remain in London, in that house, and so I moved here." Mr. Pritchard's attention flitted to the window again and the serene courtyard beyond. "It's really quite lovely."

"I understand," Fletcher murmured, compassion deepening his voice.

"Do you, Your Grace?" Mouth quirked sideways, Mr. Pritchard shook his head. "I don't think you truly can." He straightened in his chair and, after noiselessly placing both feet upon the floor, set his cup aside. "Nevertheless, it does my heart good to think another may know love at 19 Bedford Square. The house is yours if you are still interested."

"Why wouldna I be?"

Pritchard raised a cynical eyebrow.

"Och, I'm truly grateful to ye, Pritchard. I promise ye, the house and grounds will be well taken care of." Fletcher stood and extended his hand.

Mr. Pritchard also rose, and they shook hands.

"I do hope to find love and happiness there as well, Mr. Pritchard. My man of affairs will be in touch."

"If I might, I would ask one thing of you, Your Grace."

Fletcher finished straightening his jacket before glancing upward. "Aye?"

"Don't remove the wisteria. I know it's a lot of work to maintain, but Terrance loved it."

Giving a nod, Fletcher grinned. "It's grown into the plane tree. I'll only trim it enough to keep it from choking the life out of the tree. My *lèannan* also adores the vine."

"*Lèannan*?" Two neat lines puzzled Pritchard's high forehead, made more so by his thinning hair. "I'm not familiar with the word."

"It's Gaelic for sweetheart," Fletcher told him.

Was Rayne his sweetheart?

Could she be?

10

19 Bedford Square
The next day

Fletcher tapped his fingertips atop the too-small-for-his-frame but serviceable desk in the salon he'd turned into a study because it overlooked the gardens. If all went as expected, the house would legally be his by next week.

When Leith MacKettrick was assigned a task, he accomplished it with commendable haste and precision. He had every confidence his man would not fail him in this.

Once the papers were signed, Fletcher could begin the renovations and refurbishing he'd contemplated in earnest. First on the list: a new desk. One he could get his knees under without practically upending the thing.

He stopped drumming his fingers on the desk and instead balanced both elbows on the surface, creating a vee, and cradled his chin atop his folded hands. The wisteria blossoms had faded, and soon the trailing blooms would be no more.

Yesterday, he'd sent Rayne a note explaining the previous owner's fondness for the wisteria and suggested Pritchard might appreciate a sketch. Fletcher bent his mouth into a droll smile. He'd resorted to manipulation in order to see her. Though, in all fairness, he honestly did think Pritchard would value a rendering of the garden.

Perhaps it would bring the still grieving man a degree of peace.

Rayne had finally allowed Fletcher to view her drawings, and she'd blushed prettily under his praise. She possessed talent—tremendous skill—in truth.

Of its own volition, his attention gravitated to the stone wall at the garden's far end. The majestic chimneys of Sheffields' manor were visible above the treetops.

Was Rayne at home?

In the gardens?

Was she thinking of him too?

A jay perched on one of the plane tree's lower branches and arched its neck, releasing a raspy cry. With a graceful arch of its gray-brown wings, it took to the air and disappeared over the rock wall.

Upon spying a blue butterfly drifting near the wisteria, he sat up straighter.

Was it another holly blue?

Snorting, Fletcher conceded he was hopeless.

His thoughts constantly migrated to Rayne.

Tomorrow was the Gravenstones' much-touted ball. And by George, Asherford had somehow wheedled Fletcher into attending as a peacock.

A bloody, damned peacock.

In fact, all of their ducal friends had agreed to go.

"An ostentation of peacocks for an ostentatious gathering," he muttered drolly to himself.

At the awful jest, he snorted aloud again.

Each duke was to wear a peacock feather domino

and a vibrantly colored cloak—purple, green, blue, or turquoise—over their black evening attire.

Fletcher's had arrived only this morning—a shimmering aquamarine overlaid with silver and gold sequins. He couldn't help but be impressed. The color reminded him of the gown Rayne had worn that first day he'd encountered her sneaking into his garden.

Of more import, however, was that Sheffield had agreed to attend as part of the ducal alliance, and that meant Rayne would also be there. According to Sheffield, his niece disliked masked balls but had agreed to come dressed as a rose. Her first choice of costume, according to a bemused Sheffield, had been that of a nun, but the duchess had talked her out of that stark decision.

Fletcher and Rayne had shared three more clandestine meetings—all in Sheffields' gardens. She steadfastly refused to come over the wall again. He hadn't even been able to tempt her with news that the folly and surrounding area had been left naturalized.

Forcing his attention to his desk, he scowled at the neatly folded rectangle laid atop his correspondence.

He lifted the letter between his thumb and forefinger, and his grimace deepened when he recognized the looping handwriting, smelled a hint of lavender and lilac, and spied the telltale purple wax seal.

He gave a disgusted growl.

Another from his mother. One had arrived daily for a week. Twice yesterday, in fact.

Fletcher supposed she deserved credit for persistence and tenacity.

He unwaveringly refused to respond to her missives or answer her summons that he attend her at once. He'd been so infuriated at her and Lady St. Lavelle's highhandedness—and likely Cecelia's too, though she protested her innocence with tears and a lace handkerchief dabbed daintily upon her rouged cheeks—he'd almost threatened to cut Mother's funds off.

Except that meant she'd have to take up residence in the dower house. And God help him for being a wretched son, he didn't want her anywhere near Levensyde House. How a woman could birth three children so wholly opposite her in every way was beyond him.

A sharp, evenly spaced *knock, knock* at the study door broke his unpleasant reverie.

"Come."

Wofford, the newly hired footman, as stiff and formal as ever a man intent on becoming a majordomo someday had ever lived, entered.

One, two, three steps.

Heels together.

Polished shoes perfectly aligned.

Never two steps or four steps. Just three. Unless Fletcher requested Wofford to remove or bring him something. Then the man moved with the measured precision of clock hands.

Tick-step. Tock-step.

Tick-step. Tock-step.

Given MacKettrick's irregular sense of humor, he'd likely thought the austere servant a hysterical addition to the household. As had been the one-eyed gardener with a penchant for whisky, the maid with a lisp and two different colored eyes, and the flame-haired, buxom, former prostitute—now acting as

Fletcher's cook.

Just *how* recently Tildy Flanney had abandoned her previous profession, MacKettrick hadn't been precisely clear about. In fact, he'd been downright evasive.

"Your Grace, you have a visitor," Wofford elucidated in artfully practiced neutral tones. "A female visitor."

Shoulders squared impressively, Wofford looked directly ahead like a well-trained soldier. So much starch stiffened the cravat cutting into his chin, he probably had no other choice but to look forward.

Fletcher narrowed his eyes.

How *did* he manage to turn his head or to look down?

Wait.

What?

A female visitor?

The last three words finally registered fully.

Holy hell.

Fletcher tossed down the unopened letter.

His mother had dared to show her face here?

Devil take her and her audacity. The woman knew no bounds. Well, by God, she'd gone beyond the mark this time. It was far past time he set her straight and made the consequences of her meddling in his life known.

Still seething, a diatribe of unpleasant thoughts parading through his mind, Fletcher stood and pulled on his forest-green, black velvet trimmed coat. "Where is she?"

"I've taken the liberty of showing her to the floral drawing room."

As Fletcher hadn't yet fully furnished the house or seen to redecorating the slightly outdated interior, he supposed that was the wisest decision. The drawing room's carpet was faded but not threadbare. Though the furnishings were not to his taste, they weren't in poor repair.

"Shall I request a tea tray, Your Grace?"

"Nae, Wofford. She willna be here long enough to enjoy a cup of yer most excellent tea."

Wofford prided himself on his tea-making skills the way an artist took pride in a portrait. With the haughty aplomb of the Prince Regent, the servant regally lifted his nose. "Very good, Your Grace."

Fletcher could've told the loyal servant to toss the baggage waiting in the floral drawing room out on her haughty hind end, and he would have done so without a blink and the same enunciated, "Very good, Your Grace."

Marching along the corridor, Fletcher rehearsed precisely what he intended to say to his irksome mother. He'd just remembered a seldom-used—*never used, truth to tell*—cottage in Scotland she might be banished to. Just the threat of sending her there ought to be enough to curb any further interference.

Throwing the door open, he strode in. "If ye think ye can waltz into my home without prior notice…"

His words trailed away at the serene vision before him.

Rayne sat primly on the floral chintz settee, her hands folded in her lap and a basket near her feet on the floor. The primrose yellow gown she wore enhanced the coppery strands in her hair that her bonnet didn't cover. Her color high and eyes bright, she looked as lovely and fresh as a dewdrop on a rose petal.

However, at his abrupt entry, the color drained from her face, and her winsome smile faded.

A wide-eyed, pale-faced maid wearing a soft gray gown sat straight as a poker in a chair in the corner of the room. The curious servant's mouth sagged, and her eyebrows climbed high on her forehead as she looked between Fletcher and Rayne.

Back and forth. Back and forth.

Back and forth like the pendulum of a well-oiled clock.

"Och, it's ye," Fletcher offered clumsily, still slightly taken aback to see Rayne sitting in his salon when she'd been so adamant, she'd not accept his invitation. Was she here because of his request she draw the wisteria for Pritchard?

"I beg your pardon, Your Grace. I didn't think to send a note around." Her guarded focus shifted to something behind him. "I misunderstood. I thought the invitation to sketch in the gardens was an open one. You did ask that I draw the wisteria for Mr. Pritchard," she reminded him primly.

Och, so that *was* the reason. Or…perhaps it was a viable excuse she could use to explain why she was here—a benevolent act for a grieving man. No one could find fault with altruistic intentions.

What twaddle. Of course, they could find fault.

"Please forgive the interruption. I'm sure you are very busy." Glancing over her shoulder, Rayne canted her head toward the goggling maid. "Maisy, we shan't be visiting the duke's gardens today after all."

Rayne made to collect her basket and rise.

Holding his palms out in a staying motion, Fletcher advanced to meet her.

"Nae, lass. I thought ye were someone else. Please forgive my brusqueness." He lifted her hand, pulling her to her feet and lightly touched his lips to her glove-covered knuckles. She was all propriety today.

Gloves *and* a bonnet.

Was that for his benefit or to waylay any possible gossip?

"Ye are *always* welcome." He lowered his voice so the maid couldn't hear him. "Day *or* night."

Twin spots of color appeared on Rayne's cheeks, but a radiant smile wreathed her face, and she made no move to take her hand from his. "Thank you. Are you positive I'm not interrupting?"

"Never. I'll always make time for ye."

"I can come back another day," she said, glancing toward the doorway. "I just thought if I'm to draw the wisteria, I needed to do so sooner rather than later. The blossoms are already fading."

"I am positive Mr. Pritchard will be moved by your kindness," Fletcher said. He *was* positive.

"Where is His Grace? Down here? There?"

Shite.

Fletcher pointed his gaze ceilingward, begging for patience from the Almighty.

"I demand you take me to him at once."

The sound of an object smacking wood rang out. At least Fletcher hoped it was wood and not poor Wofford.

"Move aside, you great buffoon." A familiar strident female voice echoed along the corridor and filtered into the salon. "I already told you. I shan't be turned aside by a mere servant. I mean to see *my* son."

Fletcher's Mother's voice rose in pitch and volume, and he winced inwardly.

God save him.

"Rayne…?"

Before he could warn her, his mother, resplendent in a violet-and-black walking gown with matching slippers and bonnet, cruised into the room like a schooner in full sail.

Was that *another* new gown?

After he'd explicitly warned her to curtail her reckless spending? *Damn my eyes*. The woman refused to listen or consider anyone else's wishes but her own.

Her green-blue eyes, so like his own, narrowed to unbecoming, wrathful slits. The movement pleated the corners and displayed ever-deepening creases, resembling a folded fan. Her nose quivered in well-controlled rage as she took in Rayne's hand in his.

Bloody hell.

Instead of letting go, Rayne tightened her fingers around Fletcher's and jutted her adorable chin out at an endearingly mulish angle.

Had his overbearing mother at last met her match in this sweet lass?

"What is the meaning of this, Kincade?" Mother pinned her flinty, censorious glare upon Rayne and stabbed her parasol in their general direction. "*Who,* might I ask, is this chit?"

Ask all ye want, but I dinna have to answer ye.

11

And Fletcher didn't.

He remained where he was, regarding his mother with cool disdain while reminding himself she'd given birth to him. He at least owed her a modicum of respect.

"I do not know her, and *I* know *everyone* who is *anyone*," the duchess said with the arrogant air of someone who is confident of her superiority.

If she thought Fletcher would stand silently by and allow her to besmirch Rayne's character or permit her to be the target of his mother's barbed tongue, she was gravely mistaken.

The truth was, he knew next to nothing about Rayne's family other than her mother had died when she was young and, by some twist of fate, the current Duchess of Sheffield had become her guardian.

There was something about the duchess's first husband being Rayne's original guardian, but Fletcher had either forgotten the details or he'd never been privy to them. In any event, it mattered not a jot to him if Rayne were the daughter of a haberdasher and a seamstress or a blacksmith and a tavern wench.

Regardless, he'd bite off his tongue before he revealed any of that to his mother.

Unlike his mother, pedigree didn't mean two farthings to him.

"I suppose *she's* the reason you've broken precious Cecelia's heart, not to mention your own dear mother's?"

"Ye'd have to possess a heart to have it broken, Mother," he replied nonchalantly. "And Miss Wellbrook has nothin' to do with the situation with Lady Sheldon-Furnsby, which ye are well aware."

His mother didn't so much as flinch at the harsh barb or well-aimed verbal censure.

"If ye must ken, this is Miss Rayne Wellbrook.

She is the Duchess of Sheffield's niece. The Sheffields are my neighbors, and the duke is my friend and business partner. Miss Wellbrook, this is my mother, the Duchess of Kincade."

Rayne angled her head but didn't curtsy or babble some insincere drivel about being glad to make the duchess's acquaintance. *No one* was ever glad to make her acquaintance.

"Bah. You always were too sentimental and softhearted for your own good, Kincade," she scoffed, taking in the room and turning her mouth down in unrepentant disapproval. "I shall send you my decorator's contact information."

"That shan't be necessary. I have my own decorator."

Fletcher would be damned if he'd permit his mother to encroach upon this house, even if it was with something as inconsequential as the recommendation of a paint color or the positioning of a vase or portrait.

Mother's gaze slid to Rayne, and she fashioned a sardonic smile. "I'm sure you do."

"Why are you here at...?" Fletcher veered a

glance to the marble and brass mantel clock. "Half of ten?" When was the last time his mother had arisen before noon? Her reason for intruding this early in the day must be dire indeed. "What do you want?"

He didn't even strive for politesse.

"Tea and scones or crumpets would be nice. I didn't break my fast." She perched on the edge of the chair farthest from Rayne as if she were afraid the upholstery might soil her gown, or Rayne might taint her with her presence.

"Nae." Tea implied she was welcome. He hadn't left her house a fortnight ago to have her come around whenever she desired and poke her nose into his affairs at 19 Bedford Square.

Rayne tightened her fingers around his.

Wofford, his gait measured but swifter than normal, entered the drawing room. His cravat hung askew, as did his waistcoat. Several tufts of previously neatly brushed sandy-brown hair stuck out at weird angles. He attempted to right his waistcoat while looking down his considerable nose at the infuriated woman, still pointing her parasol like a sword in

Fletcher's direction.

"Please forgive my tardiness, Your Grace, as well as my failure to detain your...*guest*." His flared nostrils and the slight hesitation before the word *guest* said all that he didn't dare vocalize. "I'm unaccustomed to being pushed down the stoop stairs."

Fletcher looked aghast at his mother.

"Ye shoved him down the stairs, Mother?"

He couldn't keep the incredulity and condemnation from his voice.

Rather than look chastised or repentant, the duchess elevated her chin and pursed her lips. "He would not let me pass, so I gave him a small push. A tiny little nudge, really. One couldn't even call it a true shove. His own great size and clumsiness caused him to topple onto the pavement."

Hardly, if Wofford, who weighed at least seventeen stone, had taken a tumble. But it was just like his mother to pass the blame. She'd done that for as long as Fletcher could remember.

Filling his lungs, he willed his ballooning temper under control. "*That*, Mother, is precisely why I hired

COLLETTE CAMERON

him. That is what he is supposed to do."

He could've added that it was also Wofford's duty
to keep unwanted intruders out, but at that moment, his
gaze caught Rayne's, and he couldn't bring himself to
utter the harsh words. She'd been an unwanted
intruder, and that had turned out very well indeed.

"It is indeed, sir." Giving the duchess an indignant
look, Wofford flicked his rumpled coattails to ensure
they fell neatly into place. "Perhaps, if I may be so
bold as to suggest, Your Grace, you might inform Her
Grace that my name is not Pinheaded Penguin."

Rayne gasped, clasping her free hand to her
mouth. Her coppery brown eyes twinkled merrily, the
little flecks of gold flashing, and a musical giggle
escaped her.

At the feminine tinkle, Fletcher grinned. He'd
never heard her giggle before, and he could no more
keep the broad grin from wreathing his face than poor
Wofford could've kept the duchess from barging in
like an angry tempest.

"Wofford, I trust ye werena injured as a result of
the mishap?" Fletcher said.

166

"Wofford?" Mother wrinkled her nose. "What an odd name."

Out of all of their discourse, she chose to focus on the footman's name?

"Only my pride, sir," he pronounced in a dry monotone, sliding Fletcher's mother another acrid glance. "As there were three gentlemen, two ladies, a nurse pushing a pram, a governess with her four charges, five carriages, and an equal number of horsemen nearby when I landed on my...posterior."

His ears turned an impressive shade of scarlet.

Only a superbly observant servant would've noted such details while regaining his dignity and his feet. Wofford would make a splendid butler.

Rayne giggled again, and to Fletcher's utter astonishment, Wofford winked at her. The most uptight, stodgy excuse for a manservant he'd ever encountered—and as a duke, he'd met a good deal of them—actually winked at Rayne.

It came as no surprise that the minx had won Wofford over at their first meeting. She'd done the same to him.

"Refreshments, Your Grace?" Wofford asked, never once looking in the maid's direction. "Might I take the young lady to the kitchens as well?"

"Aye, both would be appreciated."

The perplexed maid looked to Rayne, and at her nod of approval, meekly followed Wofford from the salon.

"Mother, do have a seat on the settee," Fletcher encouraged.

"Not until you tell me why this young woman is here." Turning her nose up, she thumped her lacy black parasol upon the faded carpet. She scraped a scathing, entirely disapproving glance over Rayne.

The picture of tranquility and decorum, Rayne regarded her impassively.

Fletcher wanted to applaud her for her equanimity. Many a man and woman from the lowest commoner to the most powerful peer had wilted under his mother's fierce glare and condescending attitude. Yet Rayne stood there regal and serene. Queenly, even.

"No, Kincade, she won't do. Not at all. She has freckles on her nose," she whispered sotto voce.

Rayne remained remarkably unruffled at his mother's horrid behavior.

"Oh, and on my cheeks, chest, and *elsewhere*, Your Grace," Rayne said, a naughty gleam in her flashing bronze eyes.

"I ken she does, and I find them most captivatin'." He glanced down at Rayne, giving her a warm, reassuring smile. She was an absolute marvel. He was particularly interested in the ginger marks on her chest and elsewhere.

She must've guessed his train of thought, for pink tinged her cheeks.

Fletcher faced his mother, his patience growing ever slimmer. "Again, I must ask, why are you here, Mother?"

She leveled Rayne a frosty, contemptuous stare. "I'd prefer not to discuss it in front of Miss Wellbrook."

"She stays," he said, flint edging the two words.

"You must know, Kincade," his mother continued, cunningness slipping into her gaze and tenor. "It's not the thing to entertain a young woman in a bachelor's residence. I can only presume she's your mistress?"

At the calculated slur, Rayne stiffened, her sharp intake of breath audible in the now silent room.

"She is no' my mistress, Mother," Fletcher bit out, fury resonating in each clipped syllable.

"I'll bid you a good day, Your Grace," Rayne said to him. "I shall sketch the wisteria another time."

Dammit.

His mother's vindictive arrows had hit their intended target.

Rayne picked up her basket and, with her lashes lowered, moved past him. The brave darling stopped before his mother.

"I am not His Grace's mistress, and I resent the implication. You saw the maid who accompanied me, and even now, two footmen assigned by my guardians are standing in the garden to ensure propriety. I am only here because I agreed to draw a scene for the previous owner."

A snide smile curved his mother's mouth.

"La, could you not come up with a better excuse than that?" Once more, she took Rayne's measure, and her slightly curled upper lift indicated she'd found her wanting. "I suppose you are pretty enough if one likes ordinary and unrefined."

"Enough, Mother," Fletcher snapped, each syllable icy and cutting.

He'd throw the vicious bitch out himself if she didn't shut her cruel mouth.

She leaned forward, resting both hands atop the parasol's scrimshaw handle. "You do know, do you not, Miss Wellbrook, that my son has vowed to *only* marry a Scotswoman and never, under any circumstances, an Englishwoman? That is how I am certain you mean nothing more to him than a common harlot would."

"Enough!" he roared thunderously.

Must she pollute everything good and pure with her toxic venom?

Rayne recoiled as if struck and swung an agony-filled glance in his direction. A blink later, she masterfully donned a mask of disinterest. If Fletcher hadn't seen the hurt and accusation in her pretty eyes, he'd never have believed the regally composed woman staring his harridan of a mother down had shown any such emotion.

"As I have never entertained any idea of marrying above my station, the duke's preferences for a bride are of no interest to me, Your Grace. I'm the daughter of a soldier and an opera singer. I know my place, and it is not amongst the upper ten thousand. I am grateful my birth prohibits me from joining the ranks and spares me the company of such vile persons as yourself."

At the insult, his mother's jaw sagged to her chest, and she blinked rapidly.

Well done, Rayne.

She'd done the impossible—rendered his mother speechless.

With quiet dignity, she turned toward the door, and it struck Fletcher with the force of a claymore to the ribs.

He loved her.

God and all the saints, he loved Rayne Wellbrook. The garden nymph with her burnished hair and eyes, berry red lips, and the purest, kindest heart of any living being.

And his mother may have ruined any chance of their happiness, just as she'd intended.

"Rayne." He started after her but drew to an abrupt halt.

Goddammit.

He couldn't say what he wanted to say with his mother smugly looking on. He fisted his hands and clenched his jaw until he thought the bones might crack.

Look at me.

Dinna leave like this.

Please, let me explain.

Spine straight and proud, Rayne glided from the room without a backward glance.

"'Tis for the best, Kincade," his mother said in the patronizing manner she always adopted when she believed she'd won an argument. "She'd never do. Surely you were aware a woman of her breeding could never be the next Duchess of Kincade."

"*Her* breeding? This coming from a malicious, immoral adulteress who abandoned her children and husband? Rayne Wellbrook is far superior to you in every way, madam."

Something in his voice must've finally registered, for his mother's rouged cheeks went pale.

Icy fury tunneling through him, he stared at her. It wasn't healthy or normal to despise one's parent. The Bible said to honor your mother and father. God help him, Fletcher had tried to. Aye, but the Good Book also said for fathers not to provoke their children to anger.

After glancing at the mantel clock, he approached the duchess. When he stood three feet away, he clasped his hands behind his back. Standing there, Fletcher willed his fury to ease. After several tense moments, he could at last speak without violently cursing, he smiled. A hard, merciless, uncompromising upward sweep of his lips.

She'd brought this on herself.

"Fletcher?" Uncertainty puckered her forehead.

"Ye have exactly two hours to pack. At that time, I am personally puttin' ye in a coach, which will take ye to Aberdeen. There is a five-room cottage there that will be yer home until yer last breath. Ye may take one servant and one trunk with ye. And I do mean one. Defy me in this, and ye will no' be permitted to take any."

"Fletcher, darling." She gave an artificial laugh, one hand fluttering near her throat. Panic glinted in her eyes. "Surely you jest."

Och, so it is Fletcher now?

He couldn't recall the last time she'd addressed him by his given name. Not since he'd been a wee laddie.

"Do I look like I'm jestin'?" He withdrew his timepiece from his pocket. "One hour and fifty-six minutes."

Spluttering, her face a ghastly shade of grey beneath her cosmetics, she came unsteadily to her feet. "I understand you are upset and disappointed. But let's discuss this sensibly."

"Nae." He pounded his fist into his open palm. "Ye are a self-centered, inconsiderate woman who only cares about yerself. It wasn't enough that ye destroyed Father and deserted yer children. Ye've hurt someone I care about verra much. Someone who could make me happy. Someone who means far more to me than you ever have or ever could."

He looked to the door Rayne had disappeared through.

"If Rayne is lost to me now because of yer malicious spite, I shall never, *never* forgive ye. Ever."

Gravenstones' Ball
The next night

Heart and feet leaden, Rayne descended from the coach. She wrapped her gold-and-white satin cloak more snuggly around her as if she could ward off the stares and curious looks. Or as if she could guard her fractured heart against further pain.

Fletcher hadn't come after her. Hadn't sent a note. Hadn't sneaked into the gardens, at least she didn't think he had. She'd pleaded a headache and spent the afternoon crying, and by evening she had resolved to put him from her mind and heart.

Far, far easier said than actually done.

"You do know, do you not, Miss Wellbrook, that my son has vowed to only marry a Scotswoman and never, under any circumstances, an Englishwoman?"

Those spiteful words shredded Rayne's heart and dignity, her hopes as well, every time they replayed in her mind. Which—God curse her for a weakling—was far too often.

What had pained her far worse was when she'd turned to Fletcher, expecting him to disavow his mother's claim, and she'd seen the stark, undeniable truth reflected in his brilliant eyes.

He *had* said those very words.

That was the *what else* he'd not told her that day he'd first kissed her in the arbor. It wasn't just that he didn't want to marry Lady Cecelia Sheldon-Furnsby. Fletcher didn't want to marry *any* Englishwoman.

Oh, dallying with them, sneaking into gardens and kissing them, stealing their hearts was perfectly acceptable.

Except—

She almost missed the first step, so distracted was she. Once she was steady on her beaded satin slippers once more, she returned to her reflections. Except, she'd never have believed it of him.

How could she have been so wrong about Fletcher?

Why was he opposed to wedding an Englishwoman?

His own mother was English, for pity's sake.

For the first time in her two-and-twenty years, Rayne had not been afraid of a man who touched her. She most assuredly hadn't been revolted by Fletcher's kisses the way she had been when that fat, degenerate pig had attempted to steal her virtue in the library when she was fifteen.

A bronze candlestick thwacked on the side of his balding head had dropped Sir Lester Dryden like a boulder. From then on, whenever her uncle *entertained*, Rayne had stayed locked in her chamber, a chair propped under the door handle for good measure, and the candlestick nearby... Just in case.

She'd peek through the draperies at the arriving men and women, most of whom appeared perfectly proper and normal. But the perversions that had gone on inside Keighsdon Hall had been anything but proper and normal. Even as a young girl, she'd been aware of the hedonistic degeneracy.

More than once, those first few months, she'd gone one or two days without eating, so fearful was she of leaving her chamber until the last guest departed. She'd learned to keep a stash of non-perishable foods—nuts, apples, dried fruit, and the like—tucked into the back of her armoire for those Friday to Monday licentious revelries.

That was a polite way to describe the debauchery and depravations.

As she followed Everleigh and Griffin up the steps, Rayne kept her gaze directly ahead, her expression benign. She'd perfected indifference and was very good at disguising what went on inside her.

Hadn't she been doing so for seven years?

Initially, she'd intended to beg off attending the ball, but an inner resilience and newly found defiance wouldn't permit her to. Wouldn't allow the vindictive Duchess of Kincade to succeed in breaking her or humiliating her.

Though Rayne had been born a commoner, she possessed qualities many of the *haut ton* lacked—basic decency, for one. No one, especially someone as despicable as Fletcher's mother, would make her cringe in shame.

Rayne had no control over her humble origins, but only an idiot wouldn't feel unease about others uncovering the truth of her common birth. Others meaning the razor-tongued *ton*. Her dearest friends wouldn't care two pickles about her birth, though. That was how it should be amongst friends.

She mightn't have any influence on the behavior of other people, but she did have control over her character and how she treated others. And by God, come hell or high water, she would continue to be kind, considerate, and thoughtful.

Renewed determination winged through her, and Rayne edged her chin upward a notch.

No, she would not flee London as had been her first instinct. They—the duchess and her ilk—would not chase her away. Make her flee like a criminal.

She would stay and attend every single rout, ball,

musical, and other gatherings Everleigh and Griffin were invited to, and therefore her by default as well. Head high, she would smile and carry on as if her heart hadn't been ripped from her chest and mashed on a grinding stone.

Inhaling a fortifying breath, Rayne squared her shoulders and followed Griffin and Everleigh into the mansion. Having been warned about the garishness of the Gravenstones' palatial manor, Rayne's eyes rounded in wonderment upon entering nonetheless.

People actually lived here?

It wasn't just that the house was owned by very obviously wealthy individuals. They seemed bent on displaying that prosperity, and not tastefully either.

A grin kicked her mouth up despite her broken heart when she spied an enormous gilded peacock atop a sculpted Grecian vase on proud display in the center of the pink and black marble-floored foyer.

Griffin must've seen it too, for he stopped short, and Everleigh, dressed as Diana, goddess of the hunt, bumped into him.

Rayne was quite certain she heard him mumble,

"Holy hell. How did they know?"

Casually roving her gaze over those lingering in the massive entryway, she couldn't help but notice the attention and respect Griffin induced with his very presence.

"I beg your pardon, my dear. Please excuse my vulgarity." He placed Everleigh's hand upon his forearm. Leaning down, he murmured, "Who told them we were coming as peacocks?"

Amusement playing across her features, she lifted a shoulder. The arrows in the quiver upon her back shook slightly with the movement. "I imagine it was difficult to keep something like that a secret when all of you dukes needed cloaks and masks on such short notice."

Who would've guessed so many peers could be persuaded to don similar costumes? Griffin's cloak was a glistening midnight blue covered in gold and silver sequins. The effect was rather stunning, in truth.

Once having relinquished her cloak, Griffin escorted Rayne and Everleigh into the ballroom, and she stood blinking in wonderment. The scene before her was quite the most outlandish she'd ever seen. The ballroom and been turned into a glistening, glittering gilded forest.

Well, at least her costume was appropriate.

Multiple layers of various shades of yellow satin and silk comprised her gown. Dozens of yellow roses, as well as hundreds of clear glass beads, had been sewn onto the netted overskirt. More glass beads covered the bodice. Yellow ribbons had been threaded through her upswept hair, and she wore a wreath of yellow roses atop her head. A silk fan covered with painted yellow roses completed the costume.

Rayne was quite pleased with the result. She designed the gown herself, and though Mademoiselle Beauchêne had initially frowned at the description, she'd been all compliments and praise during Rayne's final fitting.

"Miss Wellbrook," she had said in her lyrical French accent, "if you ever want a position as a designer, come see me, *oui*?"

Rayne scanned the attendees, searching for the other ducal peacocks.

There was Asherford, heads above the other guests, and wearing a purple cloak. He turned his head this way and that as if he searched for someone.

Ophelia?

Ah, and there lounged San Sebastian against a doorframe, his cloak a pale candescent blue. There, leading his duchess onto the dance floor, was the Duke of Dandridge in a vibrant green cloak.

Each's duke's mantle shimmered and sparkled, seeming to change hues as they moved.

But Fletcher was noticeably absent.

Not wanting to examine the possible reasons why he was not here and why she should care so very much that he wasn't, Rayne took a deep breath. Her stomach unknotted a little, and when Ophelia waved to her to join her from across the ballroom, Rayne excused herself.

"I see Ophelia and Sophronie, just there," she said to her aunt, canting her head in her friends' direction.

Everleigh looked toward the two standing with a trio of other young women dressed as the three muses and nodded. "Go along, dear. Enjoy yourself."

Rayne was aware she looked particularly fetching this evening. Unlike many women, the yellow gown flattered her coloring. Most couldn't wear the shade because it made them look sallow or jaundiced.

Before, she'd never particularly cared about impressing the gentlemen. In fact, the opposite was true. She tried to remain invisible, but tonight she had something to prove to herself. Fear would no longer control her.

Smiling and relishing her newfound confidence, Rayne wound her way to Ophelia and Sophronie.

A simply radiant Nicolette Twistleton waved at them from the middle of the ballroom floor where she danced with the Duke of Westfall, attired in a coral cloak, overset with sequins just like the other dukes' cloaks.

"Why, Rayne, you are positively stunning." Ophelia eyed Rayne's gown up and down approvingly.

Ophelia was dressed all in black with myriads of silver beads and sequins.

"I'm midnight," she said, gesturing to her gown and then the jet and silver beads adorning her hair and mask.

"Very clever," Rayne said sincerely.

Sophronie Slater smoothed her hands over her unusual soft leather gown with beautifully colored beads dangling from the sleeves and hem. She wore a sort of soft leather boot that laced up her calves, and she'd braided her strawberry blonde hair. More beads and strips of leather adorned the ends of her braids.

"This really isn't a costume but a gift from a very special friend of mine in America," she said. "She-Who-Walks-Softly and I have been friends practically our whole lives. She gave me this gown as a parting gift before Papa and I sailed to England."

"It's quite lovely," Rayne said, running a finger over Sophronie's sleeve. "I've never seen any fabric like this."

"It's deerskin," Sophronie supplied.

Ophelia caught the end of a leather strip tied to one of Sophronie's braids between her fingertips. "It's so soft."

Rayne hadn't seen Ophelia since supper the other night. They'd managed to find a quiet corner to speak privately, and Rayne had admitted to Fletcher's wink. Ophelia had then confessed that Asherford had approached her about a marriage of convenience.

It was time he married and produced an heir. That was exactly what he'd said to Ophelia by way of a proposal.

She'd refused his offer by dumping her lemonade upon his expensive suit.

The utter boor.

"I believe Asherford is looking for you, Ophelia," Rayne told her friend.

Ophelia glanced over Rayne's shoulder, and her expression hardened. "Speak of the devil," she muttered beneath her breath. "Hurry, let's find our way to the ladies' retiring room."

"Too late," Sophronie whispered, pasting a false smile upon her face.

Ah, so Ophelia had confided in her as well.

Rayne turned around, prepared to be civil but perhaps not overly warm to Asherford. After all, he'd insulted one of her dearest friends. Her attention fell on the slightly shorter man beside him. Fletcher was tall, but Asherford was taller. Her heart stalled before it resumed beating double time.

"Good evening, ladies," Asherford said, nodding.

Rayne had to admit the men looked dashing with their peacock feather dominos and gleaming cloaks. From the envious looks directed their way by numerous other ladies present, they thought so as well.

"May I have this dance, Miss Wellbrook?" Fletcher said, extending his hand. His cloak was a magnificent aquamarine shade that did fantastical things to his eyes. Things she had no business noticing.

Rayne had every intention of refusing him. Not only because wisdom and a bruised heart dictated that was the wisest course of action, but how could she leave Ophelia to Asherford's mercies?

She needn't have worried about her friend.

Ophelia pasted a brilliant smile upon her face and promptly agreed to dance with Neville Hornbrook. Never mind that the painfully shy and awkward banker hadn't actually asked Ophelia to dance.

Before Rayne could comprehend what had happened, Ophelia had towed the beet-faced banker halfway to the dancefloor. Over her shoulder, she shot a rather smug, I'd-rather-dance-with-this-tongue-tied-fool-than-you smile toward Asherford.

"Miss Wellbrook?" Fletcher's hand remained outstretched, a mischievous half-smile bending his mouth.

Rayne was caught, and the rogue well knew it. If she refused to dance with him, she couldn't dance the rest of the evening. Blast his pigheadedness and his perverse sense of amusement.

She summoned a smile—it might've been a tad bit brittle—and laid her yellow gloved hand upon Fletcher's palm. The orchestra struck the first chords, and she nearly groaned aloud.

She hadn't had the opportunity to glance at her dance card yet, but the unmistakable strains of a waltz began.

With that same masculine grace that had first snared her attention, Fletcher guided her onto the sanded floor. He took her into his arms, and Rayne blinked back tears as memories of their kisses washed over her.

"Why must you torment me, Your Grace?" she asked, needing to take control else she would dissolve into a humiliating puddle. "Haven't you toyed with me enough?"

God, when Fletcher touched her, she wanted to burrow into him. To inhale his scent and tell him of the love she'd tried to deny. The love she'd never be able to confess now.

"*Lèannan*, I would never deliberately hurt ye. Ye are too precious to me."

And *thunk*, there dropped another piece of her already fractured heart at his feet. Yes, she was an utter and complete nitwit.

Fletcher drew her closer, not scandalously so, but slightly more than was entirely proper. His essence surrounded her, comforting and familiar. He put his mouth near her ear.

"I sent my mother away yesterday. To Aberdeen. She'll never have the opportunity to cause ye pain again."

What?

Stumbling, Rayne glanced upward. He easily

steadied her and made a skillful turn. For a man his size, he possessed grace and agility.

"Why? Because of what she said to me?" She puzzled her brow. "Fletcher, she's your mother. She only wants what is best for you."

The words nearly strangled Rayne, but she'd vowed to be kind. Speaking charitably about the Duchess of Kincade so soon after her horrid behavior toward Rayne tested her mettle, however.

"Nae, she's only ever cared about herself." His words came low and hoarse. As if saying them aloud caused him pain.

He spun her in a circle, and she followed his lead. Never had dancing come so easily. Typically, she was a nervous wreck and spent every moment concentrating on not casting up her accounts on her partner's glossy shoes.

Roving her gaze over his face, she tried to memorize each dear contour and angle. His earlier vow to remain in London now seemed impossible with him living next door. She'd return to Fittledale Park rather than torment herself with the knowledge he was just over the garden wall, and yet he might as well be across the ocean.

Tears stung behind her eyelids, and she lowered her lashes lest he see.

"Rayne?"

God, how she adored his brogue and the melodious way her name flowed off his tongue.

She wouldn't look up. Couldn't look into his eyes. He'd see her love for him, and she didn't think she could bear his pity.

"Rayne. Look at me."

She shook her head. "No."

It wasn't until the cool breeze caressed her bare shoulders that she realized he'd whisked them onto the terrace. She gazed about, half-stunned, but relieved to see several other people meandering along the veranda. At least her reputation would remain intact.

Not so, her heart.

"What are you doing?" she whispered, attempting to tug her hand from his.

"Tryin' to apologize and beg yer forgiveness."

Sighing, Rayne looked past his broad shoulder

into the lantern-lit garden. "What's there to forgive, Fletcher? I willingly kissed you. You never made any promises." Somehow, she fashioned a genuine smile. "I'm not angry. Truly, I understand. I'm English and a commoner, to boot."

That didn't mean, however, that she had to like it. But she did understand.

"Ye dinna understand anythin', and I shall explain all later. But for now, all ye need to ken is I love ye, lass. Love ye so much, I canna see any future without ye in it. I want to marry ye, Rayne. If ye'll have me."

Blistering tears sprang to her eyes once more, and the veriest morsel of hope took wing, flitting about her chest like a tiny insect. "But I'm English. Your mother said—"

"I dinna want to marry an Englishwoman like *her*."

At some point, they'd stopped dancing, and he'd maneuvered them into a secluded corner.

"She abandoned my father and her three children eighteen years ago. Her only interest in me, my brother, and my sister is what she can gain from a relationship with us. I could no' join myself to a woman like that for a lifetime. That is why I dinna want to marry a cold English aristocrat."

"Oh."

It made perfect sense.

He'd been afraid. This big, strong, wonderful man had been afraid.

A roguish but infinitely tender grin arched his mouth at what must've been her stupefied expression.

He brushed his bent forefinger over her cheek. "What say ye, my yellow English rose? Will ye take this rough Scotsman as yer husband? We'll have our rough moments, I've nae doubt, but if I love ye and ye love me…"

A scowl pulled his midnight brows together.

"Ye do love me, dinna ye, Rayne?"

"How can you doubt it? I fell in love with you that first day in your garden." Standing on her tiptoes, Rayne pulled his mouth down to meet hers, but he resisted her urging.

"I dinna want a long engagement. Marry me by special license, and we'll honeymoon in Scotland."

"My, but *you* are in a hurry."

"Aye, I dinna want to take a chance of losin' ye ever again." He wrapped his arms around her waist and pulled her into the vee of his strapping legs. The evidence of his affection was quite apparent.

As his lips brushed hers, Rayne whispered, "How soon can you get a special license?"

Fletcher's laugher filled the night air, certain to draw attention.

And for once, Rayne didn't care a jot about her reputation.

Epilogue

Levensyde House
July 1818

Holding her three-year-old daughter, Bailey, Rayne stood at the top of the porch observing the tableau before her. A slight breeze ruffled her skirt and her unbound hair. She seldom fashioned the long tresses into a knot. Fletcher preferred she wear her hair down, and there was nothing she loved more than pleasing her husband, except perhaps their children.

Coatless, his midnight hair gleaming in the sun, Fletcher slowly led the rust-colored Shetland pony around the courtyard. Their four-year-old son, Brixton, giggled and clutched the pony's creamy mane.

"Look at me, Mama," he cried. "I'm ridin' a wee horsie."

"That's a wee pony," his older brother Channing corrected. He rode his own pony and, in typical older brother fashion, showed off his skills by trotting Marmaduke across the green.

"Be careful, Channing," Rayne called with motherly concern.

Fletcher glanced up. Even after eight years of marriage and three children—soon to be four—his hot gaze still sent her pulse cavorting. He grinned and handed the reins off to the young groom. "Take it slowly, Robbie. Brixton needs to become accustomed to the movement."

To think she'd told Ophelia all those years go in Hyde Park that she wanted more than *just* marriage. This marriage to Fletcher was more satisfying and fulfilling than anything she could've ever have imagined. Not only did he include her in his business discussions, but Rayne had decided being a wife and mother was very rewarding indeed.

"Aye, Yer Grace." The groom, Robbie Gazley,

nodded and, with a wink at Brixton, took over the riding lesson.

Fletcher trotted up the steps. When he reached Rayne, Bailey stretched her arms out. "Papa, hold me."

If ever there was a daddy's girl, it was Bailey. She possessed her father's raven hair and blue-green eyes as well. The boys' hair was darker than Rayne's but lighter than Fletcher's. Both had inherited jade-green eyes from their paternal grandfather.

"I had a letter from Greg today," Fletcher said before brushing his lips across Bailey's crown. "He's in Cairo and says he is making great progress with the spice merchants."

Greg had eagerly taken Fletcher up on the offer to supervise his overseas operations. The change of location and clime had done him a world of good. He'd married the daughter of a diplomat, and they had no plans to return to Scotland anytime soon.

After two Seasons, Florence had returned to Dumfries and married the local vicar. She was expecting their second child as well. Fletcher had forgiven his mother, but not enough to permit her to live in the dower house.

Instead, he'd bought her a lovely cottage in Brighton, permitted her three servants, and paid her a visit once a year. She wrote on occasion but had never forgiven him for marrying beneath his station.

Fletcher drew Rayne into his strong embrace with his free arm. "How are ye feelin'?"

He eyed her distended belly.

"Like a great brood cow." Laughing, she smoothed her palms over her swollen stomach. This baby wasn't due for six weeks, but familiar twinges had begun yesterday.

"I had a letter from Theadosia," she said. Thea was already eagerly planning the annual Christmastide gathering at Ridgewood Court. Each year she somehow managed to outdo the year before. "We will go, won't we?"

He grinned and kissed her forehead. "We havena missed a year yet, love."

Nearly all of the people who'd attended the first Christmas house party also made an effort to attend annually. And all were married now as well. Rayne had long ago begun suspecting Theadosia had missed her calling as a matchmaker.

A spasm low in her back made Rayne wince. Arching her spine, she pressed her hand to the small of her back. A gush of warm water spilled down her legs, pulling a startled gasp from her.

Well, this baby was going to put in an early appearance, it seemed.

"Fletcher?"

"Hmm?" he replied distractedly as he observed their sons' progress on the ponies.

"Please send Gazley for Dr. Pepperidge."

Fletcher's gaze whipped to hers—his eyes intense and questioning—then dipped to her tummy. "But... But the bairn isna due for weeks yet."

"I don't think the baby knows how to tell time." She looked pointedly at the pool surrounding her feet.

"Gazley," Fletcher roared, his face pale as chalk.

Poor man.

Rayne wasn't sure if delivering their bairns was harder on her or her husband.

The groom jerked his head up, worry and

confusion stamped upon his face.

"Go for Dr. Pepperidge." Fletcher threw a frantic glance at the puddle surrounding Rayne's feet. "Now!"

After a panicked glance toward Rayne's soaked skirts, Robbie bobbed his head. "Aye, Yer Grace." He swiftly removed Brixton and Channing from their mounts and then, leading the ponies by their reins, set off toward the stables at a full sprint.

The poor ponies lumbered behind him on their stubby little legs.

The next twelve hours were a flurry of activity. After kissing each of her children on their impossibly soft cheeks and explaining they'd soon have a new brother or sister, Rayne gratefully sought her bed.

The doctor arrived and went about the preparations for the impending birth. Water was boiled, linens prepared, and the household waited with bated breath as Rayne labored to birth another McQuinton.

Since Channing's birth, Fletcher had refused to leave her side while she strove to bring their children into the world. He pressed cool cloths to her forehead, murmured words of encouragement and comfort, and held her hand throughout it all.

At ten minutes of one in the morning, Liliana McQuinton made a squalling entrance into the world. And at two minutes of one, Lyle McQuinton quietly slid into his father's hands.

Grinning from ear to ear, Fletcher held up the still bloody baby. "Twins, *lèannan*. A lass and a laddie."

"Well done, ye, Yer Grace." Dr. Pepperidge gave a nod of approval. "Both bairns are the picture of health." Wiping his hands on the cloth a maid had provided, he looked to Fletcher. "Congratulations, Yer Grace."

"Thank ye, Doctor," Fletcher said, his voice tight with suppressed emotion.

A tear trickled from the corner of Rayne's eyes. Exhausted but happier than she'd ever been, she said, "I didn't know twins ran in your family, Fletcher."

"They dinna, as far as I ken." Fletcher chuckled. "It must be from yer side."

An hour later, having nursed both of her newborns, and the babes having been bundled away by grinning, cooing nurses, Rayne sagged against the clean linens. Fletcher crawled into bed and gently took her into the circle of his arms.

"Are ye in pain, darlin'?"

Rayne thought for a moment then shook her head. "Not really. I'm sore, of course, but not any more so than the other births."

"I love ye, Rayne." He tipped her chin up so that their eyes met. "Ye've brought me more happiness and joy than I ever believed possible. Thank God ye trespassed that day, and I met ye."

Snuggling into his side and laying her head on his bare chest, she played with the crisp black hair there. "I think we would've met eventually, one way or another. We were meant to be together."

"Aye, that we were. For now and forever."

He sealed that vow with a tender kiss.

About the Author

USA Today Bestselling, award-winning author COLLETTE CAMERON® scribbles Scottish and Regency historicals featuring dashing rogues and scoundrels and the intrepid damsels who reform them.Blessed with an overactive and witty muse that won't stop whispering new romantic romps in her ear, she's lived in Oregon her entire life, though she dreams of living in Scotland part-time. A self-confessed Cadbury chocoholic, you'll always find a dash of inspiration and a pinch of humor in her sweet-to-spicy timeless romances®.

Explore **Collette's worlds** at
www.collettecameron.com!

Join her **VIP Reader Club** and **FREE newsletter**.
Giggles guaranteed!

FREE BOOK: Join Collette's The Regency Rose®
VIP Reader Club to get updates on book releases,
cover reveals, contests, and giveaways she reserves
exclusively for email and newsletter followers. Also,
any deals, sales, or special promotions are offered to
club members first. She will not share your name or
email, nor will she spam you.

http://bit.ly/TheRegencyRoseGift

Follow Collette on BookBub
https://www.bookbub.com/authors/collette-cameron

From the Desk of Collette Cameron

Thank you for reading THE DEBUTANTE AND THE DUKE.

I adore Scottish Regencies or Regencies with a Scottish main character. They combine my two most favorite genres. If you've read the other books in my SEDUCTIVE SCOUNDRELS SERIES, you've seen Rayne mentioned a few times. For those who might be concerned about the historical authenticity of her given name, Rayne dates back to at least the fifteenth century.

In THE DEBUTANTE AND THE DUKE, Rayne tells Fletcher her name means song. That is the Scandinavian, Israeli meaning of the name. More commonly, you'll find references to the name in the medieval era and it is derived from *reine or* "queen." In Old French, *raine* meant frog, and in Aberdeenshire, Scotland, there is a place called Rayne, which means a strip of land.

As it often does, my muse knew more about her

than I did. When I decided she'd love singing because her mother had been an opera singer, I didn't know the name Rayne meant song, amongst other things. That happens so often in my writing now that I have to believe a higher force is guiding me. While Rayne is not an outgoing, strong, independent female lead, she is courageous and intrepid in her own way. She doesn't feel the need to prove herself to anyone, and I admire that in her.

Fletcher is the quintessential hero, in my opinion: confident, sensitive, and possessing a flirty sense of humor. I tried to create a believable conflict between him and his overbearing mother. People who have warm, loving parents can struggle with understanding dysfunctional child/parent relationships or a parent portrayed as a villain. Unfortunately, they are all too real and far more common than any of us wants to believe.

You may have noticed several references to Ophelia Breckensole and the Duke of Asherford, as well as Sophronie Slater and the Duke of Waycross in THE DEBUTANTE AND THE DUKE. Their stories release soon.

Please consider telling other readers why you enjoyed this book by reviewing it. I also truly adore hearing from my readers. You can contact me on my website, collettecameron.com, and while you are there, explore my author world. If you enjoyed reading Rayne and Fletcher's story, be sure to check out the other books in my SEDUCTIVE SCOUNDRELS SERIES.

Hugs,

Collette

Look for book 12 in the Seductive Scoundrels series!

Earl of Keyworth

The only thing redeemable about the enigmatic and aloof Landry, Earl of Keyworth, was his giant dog. Never had a man infuriated Celestia Tolman more. After the bounder nearly bankrupted her father, Celestia decided to take matters into her own hands. She'd teach the arrogant lord a lesson he'd never forget.

There were two things in all the world that Landry couldn't abide: liars and cheaters. So when the delectable bluestocking, Celestia Tolman, shows up on his doorstep and attempts to sway his sympathies in favor of her charlatan of a father, Landry has no patience. He sends her packing.

Then the ugly rumors began to circulate about him, and he need look no further than the green-eyed temptress who'd vowed vengeance for her father and their family honor.

CPSIA information can be obtained
at www.ICGtesting.com
Printed in the USA
LVHW050348120121
676187LV00005B/216